The room w̲
belonged there, which was absolutely

Karly turned to go back into the kitchen to wait for Blake, and walked right into his broad chest. Stumbling backward, she would have fallen if not for his big hands encircling her upper arms to steady her.

"I'm sorry. I didn't mean to—"

Her voice failed her as she gazed up into his sexy brown eyes, and for a split second, she thought she caught a glimpse of the warm, compassionate man she'd thought she was in love with. But just as quickly as it appeared, the glimmer was gone, replaced by a closed-off stare.

"You'd better watch your step," he said, his deep baritone sending a shiver coursing through her. "One of these days those ridiculous shoes are going to cause you to fall and break an ankle."

Before she could find her voice and tell him that she didn't need his input on what she should or shouldn't wear, he released her and motioned toward a door across the room.

"Let's go into the office for this talk you seem to think is so important."

She took a deep breath and followed him. Now she had to find a way to tell him she was still his wife.

Dear Reader,

A few years ago, I introduced you to Blake Hartwell, the best friend of the hero in my book *In the Rancher's Arms*. So many of you wrote to tell me how much you loved Blake and wanted to read his story that, this month, I'm happy to be bringing you his book.

When Blake ran into Karly Ewing in a Las Vegas hotel lobby, he bought her a drink to apologize for his carelessness. By the end of the day, they were lovers. By the end of the week, they were married. And by the end of the next week, they were filing for divorce.

In *The Rancher's One-Week Wife* we take a look at what happens when a couple who think they're divorced find out they're not only still married, but that they still can't seem to keep their hands off each other. Unfortunately, they both have secrets that could very well make finding their happily-ever-after impossible.

Sometimes rocky, sometimes filled with unexpected detours, the road to love is never easy. But it's always worth the journey.

All the best,

Kathie DeNosky

KATHIE DeNOSKY

THE RANCHER'S ONE-WEEK WIFE

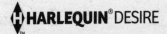

Recycling programs
for this product may
not exist in your area.

ISBN-13: 978-0-373-73480-1

The Rancher's One-Week Wife

Copyright © 2016 by Kathie DeNosky

Printed in U.S.A.

www.Harlequin.com

Kathie DeNosky lives in her native Southern Illinois on the land her family settled in 1839. Her books have appeared on the *USA TODAY* bestseller list and received numerous awards, including two National Readers' Choice Awards. Readers may contact Kathie by emailing Kathie@kathiedenosky.com. They can also visit her website, kathiedenosky.com, or find her on Facebook at Facebook.com/Kathie-DeNosky-Author/278166445536145.

Books by Kathie DeNosky

Harlequin Desire

The Rancher's One-Week Wife

The Good, the Bad and the Texan

His Marriage to Remember
A Baby Between Friends
Your Ranch...Or Mine?
The Cowboy's Way
Pregnant with the Rancher's Baby
Tempted by the Texan

Visit her Author Profile page at Harlequin.com, or kathiedenosky.com, for more titles.

This book is dedicated to my editor, Stacy Boyd.
Thank you for being my cheerleader
and for waving those pom-poms
when I need them the most.

One

Blake Hartwell shook his head in disgust when he heard the low-slung sports car bottom out in first one, then another of the many potholes pitting the dirt lane leading up to the foreman's cottage. As he brushed the sorrel gelding he'd tied to the side of the corral, he decided right then and there that whoever was behind the steering wheel of that little red toy couldn't be from the area. Folks in rural Wyoming had better sense than to drive a vehicle that sat that low on unpaved mountain roads. It was a surefire way to knock a hole in the oil pan or tear up the exhaust system on a car.

"Whoever he is, he'd better be prepared to hitch a ride on the back of an antelope if he breaks down because I'm not driving his fool hide back to town," Blake muttered as he glanced at the afternoon sun sinking toward the taller peaks to the west.

The car stopped at the side of the foreman's cottage next to Blake's truck. When the driver's door opened, a leggy blonde stepped out, causing his heart to stall and the breath to lodge in his lungs.

Blake clenched the grooming brush he'd been using on Boomer so tightly he wouldn't have been surprised if he left his fingerprints in the wood. He swallowed hard as he watched her walk toward the corral as fast as her spiked heels would allow on the uneven ground.

Slender and sleek in her formfitting black dress, her delicate body moved much like a jungle panther on the prowl. Blake's lower body tightened and he wasn't sure if it was in response to the sight of her now, or the memory of how those long legs felt wrapped around him when they made love.

"Aw, hell," he cursed under his breath. "What does *she* want?"

Boomer stamped one of his front hooves,

then looked over his shoulder as if to ask if Blake knew her.

Reminding himself to exhale, Blake released the breath he'd been holding and went back to brushing the gelding's rust-colored hide. He knew her all right. Back in December, he'd met Karly Ewing in Las Vegas. She'd been on vacation from her job—whatever that was—and he'd been in town to compete in the national bull-riding finals. He'd accidently bumped into her in the lobby at Caesar's Palace and barely managed to catch her before she fell. As a way of apologizing for his carelessness, he'd convinced her to let him buy her a drink. They'd ended up talking for hours and the chemistry between them had been explosive. By the end of the day they'd been lovers. By the end of the week they'd been husband and wife. And one week after that, they'd been filing for a divorce.

When she stopped a few feet from the horse, she looked a little uncertain, as if she wasn't sure what kind of reception she'd get from him. "H-hello, Blake."

Her voice flowed over him like a fine piece of silk and reminded him of the way it had sounded when she'd said his name as he pleasured her. Blake gritted his teeth against the heat building in his lower belly and continued to brush Boomer.

He wasn't about to let her get to him. Not again. It had taken months after that fateful phone call on New Year's Eve, when she told him she wanted a divorce, for him to get a decent night's sleep. If possible, he'd just as soon avoid repeating that.

She'd made the choice to end things between them and although he hadn't agreed with her, he had accepted it. The way he saw it, there wasn't anything they hadn't already covered and there was no sense in rehashing it now.

"What brings you to the Wolf Creek Ranch, Karly?" Without waiting for an answer, he added, "Eight months ago you weren't even willing to come here to see it. In fact, you said you weren't the least bit interested in learning anything about the backside of no-man's-land."

As long as he lived, he would never forget the sting of her rejection, or her scorn for the land he loved. The ranch had been in his family for the past hundred and fifty years and he'd spent the majority of his adult life trying to get it back from his gold-digging stepmother after his father's death. He'd finally accomplished that goal almost two years ago and once he'd made Karly his wife, he'd been looking forward to showing her the place that he was proud to call home. But she hadn't cared enough about him or it to even see the place before she refused to live there with him.

Meeting her startled gaze head-on, he did his best to ignore the effect she had on him whenever he looked into her incredible blue eyes. "Why the sudden interest in a place you had no desire to learn anything about?"

Color rose on her cheeks and it seemed as if she might be slightly embarrassed. "I, um, I'm sorry if I left you with the wrong impression, Blake. It's not that I didn't think the ranch would be beautiful…"

When her voice trailed off as she looked around, Blake stopped grooming the gelding and rested his forearms on the gentle animal's broad back to give her an expectant look. "Then what was it?"

As he stared at her, awaiting an answer, a slight breeze fluttered her long, honey-colored hair and reminded him how the silky strands had felt when he'd threaded his fingers through them as he kissed her. His body came to full arousal and he was damn glad the horse stood between them. At least she wouldn't be able to see the evidence of how he still burned for her.

Turning back to face him, her eyes couldn't

quite meet his. "I've always lived in the city and I was…" She shook her head. "It doesn't matter."

"What are you doing here, Karly?" Seeing her again was heaven and hell rolled into one neat little bundle, and the sooner she laid her cards on the table and went back to Seattle, the sooner he could get back to the business of trying to forget her.

When she took a deep breath, he did his best to ignore the rise and fall of her perfect breasts. "We need to talk, Blake."

He shook his head. "I don't know what you think we need to discuss now. We pretty much covered everything that needed to be said eight months ago. I wanted you to give us a chance to make our marriage work. You didn't want that. End of story."

"Please, Blake." She took a step back when Boomer blew out a gentle breath through his nose and turned his head to gaze at her. Looking a little apprehensive, she continued. "I wouldn't be here if it wasn't important. Could we please go somewhere we can sit down and talk? I promise I won't take up too much of your time."

Blake sighed heavily. It was clear she wasn't going anywhere until she'd said her piece.

KATHIE DeNOSKY 13

And truth to tell, he did need to talk to her. He hadn't yet received a copy of their divorce papers and he needed them for his records.

"The door's open," he finally said, motioning toward the foreman's cottage. "Make yourself at home. I'll be in as soon as I put Boomer in his stall for the night."

She opened her mouth as if she intended to say something more, then with a short nod she turned on her black spiked heels and slowly walked toward the back porch. Watching the gentle sway of her slender hips as she navigated the hard-packed, uneven ground in those ridiculous shoes, Blake shifted his weight from one foot to the other in an effort to relieve the pressure in his now too-tight jeans. He'd spent the past eight months trying to forget how her soft curves had felt beneath his hands and how her kisses were the sweetest this side of heaven. Seeing her here—where he'd wanted her—was bringing back all the memories he thought he'd left behind.

Shaking his head, he untied the gelding's lead rope from the top fence rail. He had no idea what she thought they needed to discuss, but if it had brought her from Seattle all the way to his remote ranch in Wyoming, it had to be pretty damn important.

Leading Boomer into the barn, he decided to get this meeting over with as soon as possible. Then, after he watched Karly drive off his land and away from him for good, he had every intention of getting his brother, Sean, to come over from his ranch on the other side of the mountain and go with him to the Silver Dollar Bar in the tiny community of Antelope Junction. Sean could be the designated driver, while Blake finally finished the job of forgetting he'd ever met the petite blonde who'd turned his world upside down from the moment he'd laid eyes on her.

Karly opened the back door to Blake's home and walked into the kitchen on shaky legs. It had taken every ounce of courage she possessed to face him again, and although she had thought she'd put their brief relationship in perspective and moved on, his effect on her had been no less devastating today than it had been eight months ago, when she'd agreed to become his wife.

Blake was every bit as handsome, every bit as masculine and even sexier than she'd remembered. With wide shoulders, narrow hips and long muscular legs, he had a physique women drooled over and men spent endless hours in a gym trying to attain. But the steely muscles covering his tall frame had been honed from years of ranch work and competing in rodeos, not from lifting weights or working out on fitness machines. He was the real deal—the epitome of every woman's cowboy fantasy, and then some.

That was something she hadn't even realized she possessed until they ran into each other in Las Vegas. But when he caught her to him to keep her from falling, all it had taken was one look at the cowboy holding her to his wide chest and she'd come close to melting into a puddle at his big-booted feet.

A delicious little shiver slid up her spine when she remembered how it had felt to be held in his strong arms, to taste the passion of his masterful kiss and experience the power of his desire as he made love to her. Her breathing grew shallow and her heart sped up. She forced herself to ignore it.

The hardest thing she'd ever done had been making the call to tell Blake she thought it would be in both of their best interest to call off their brief marriage. But when she had returned home, she'd thought about how little they knew about each other and she couldn't think of a single thing thcy had in common

besides not being able to keep their hands off
of each other. Her breath caught and she had
to swallow hard against the sudden wave of
emotion threatening to overtake her.

"Get a grip," she admonished herself. "Nothing has changed. He lives here and you live in
Seattle. It would have never worked."

To distract herself, she glanced around
Blake's neatly kept home. Even though the
appliances were ultramodern, the rest of the
kitchen appeared to be as rugged and masculine as the man who lived there.

A wooden butcher-block island sat in the
middle of the kitchen with a variety of copper
bottom skillets, pots and pans hanging above
it from a wrought-iron rack. The cabinets were
a warm oak with hammered black hinges and
door pulls; the countertop was polished blue
marble. A wagon wheel suspended from the
ceiling with old-fashioned-looking chimney
lamps served as a chandelier over the round
oak dining table, while the windows on the
wall behind the dining area framed a panoramic view of the Laramie Mountains, which
surrounded the ranch.

"Beautiful," she murmured as she gazed at
the picture-perfect landscape. It was as rugged
and fascinating as the man she was here to see.

Wandering into the living room, she wasn't at all surprised to see a stone fireplace with a rough-hewn mantel surrounded by a grouping of heavy leather furniture and rustic wooden end tables. The room was so cozy and inviting, she felt as if she belonged there, which was absolutely ridiculous. She belonged in Seattle, in her own apartment with its modern decor and view of the city. And try as she might, she couldn't imagine how it would have been living here with Blake. If that wasn't enough to convince her that she'd made the right decision, she didn't know what was.

But as she looked around at the colorful Native American throws on the back of the large leather sofa, and the pieces of vintage tack and Western accents hanging on the walls, she had to admit that Blake's home had a warm, friendly feel to it that her place had never possessed. An uncharacteristic loneliness suddenly invaded every part of her. She did her best to tamp it down.

She loved her life in Seattle. She had a great job as buyer for a large import/export dealer and although she didn't have much of a social life, she did occasionally go out with some of her coworkers for happy hour after work. But as she thought about how long it had been since that had happened, she took a deep breath. She really couldn't say she had a lot in common with any of them anymore. They were all either married or in committed relationships and were more interested in going home to their significant others than hanging out to talk shop.

It was odd she hadn't noticed that before she met Blake. And she had to admit that when she did realize it, she might have had second thoughts about her decision to end things with him. In the end, she hadn't let that sway her and resigned herself to being the only one in her office with no one to go home to.

But the more she thought about it, the more her loneliness increased. Shaking her head to dislodge the unsettling feeling, Karly turned to go back into the kitchen to wait for Blake and walked right into his broad chest. Stumbling backward, she would have fallen if not for his big hands encircling her upper arms to steady her.

"I'm sorry. I didn't mean to—"

Her voice failed her as she gazed up into his sexy brown eyes. For a split second, she thought she caught a glimpse of the warm, compassionate man she'd thought she was in love with. But just as quickly as it appeared the glimmer was gone, replaced by a closed-off stare.

"You'd better watch your step," he said, his deep baritone sending a shiver coursing through her. "One of these days those ridiculous shoes are going to cause you to fall and break an ankle." Before she could find her voice and tell him that she didn't need his input on what she should or shouldn't wear, he released her and motioned toward a door across the room. "Let's go into the office for this talk you seem to think is so important."

Blake stepped back for her to precede him into a study off the living room, and as she seated herself in the burgundy leather armchair in front of his desk, Karly forced herself to stay calm. The heat from his calloused palms through the fabric of her dress when he caught her had set her pulse racing and made breathing all but impossible.

She tried to calm herself as she stared at the outdoor scene intricately carved into the oak desk's front panel. She'd just as soon face off with the bear fishing in the stream as she would having to deliver the news she'd traveled over a thousand miles to give Blake.

"So what brings you all the way to Wyoming, Karly?" He removed his hat and hung it on a peg by the door. "I'm betting you didn't make this trip by choice."

He wasn't going to make their meeting easy and she really hadn't expected him to. When they'd decided to dissolve their marriage eight months ago, they had both said things out of hurt and frustration that she was sure they both regretted.

"Please, Blake. Can't we at least—"

"What do you expect from me, Karly?" he interrupted, sinking into the chair behind his desk. "I haven't seen or heard from you since just before the first of the year. After we spent Christmas in Las Vegas, I came home expecting my wife to be joining me here for New Year's Eve. Instead, I get a call telling me you'd changed your mind. If I wanted to stay married, I'd have to give up my life on the Wolf Creek Ranch, quit riding bulls and move to Seattle because you decided you couldn't live out in the middle of nowhere."

"That isn't exactly what I told you," she said, defending herself.

"Close enough," he stated flatly.

"You were just as adamant that you couldn't live in the city," she reminded him, feeling a little guilty. He hadn't been as insulting in his assessment of Seattle as she'd been about where the ranch was located. But dredging up what he said and what she said wasn't getting to the point of her visit. When they continued to glare at each other for what seemed an eternity, she sighed and shook her head. "I didn't come here to argue with you, Blake."

"Why *are* you here? I thought we settled things when I signed the papers without contesting the divorce." He frowned. "By the way, I'd like to get a copy of the final decree. You said your lawyer was supposed to mail that to me, but like everything else you promised, it didn't happen."

Karly stared down at her tightly clasped hands. She supposed he was right. She had made several promises that she hadn't been able to keep. She'd meant to keep them at the time. But once she went back home to pack her things and close her apartment, her sanity returned and the fear of failure had her second-guessing everything that had happened in Las Vegas.

"When I took the documents back to Mr. Campanella after you signed them, he suggested that I file for the divorce myself in Lincoln County on the eastern side of the state," she finally said. "Which I did."

Blake frowned. "Why?"

"The dockets in Seattle are filled with other domestic matters and it can take up to a year or more just to get a court date," she explained. "All I had to do was mail the signed documents to the courthouse in Lincoln County and after the ninety-day cooling-off period the divorce would be final."

"Mail them?" His frown darkened. "I thought a lawyer and at least one of the petitioners had to go before a judge for a divorce. At least that's how I think it is here. Is it different in Washington State?"

Rubbing her temples, Karly tried to concentrate. This was what she'd come here to tell him. It was also where everything got extremely complicated. "If the petition had been filed in Seattle, Mr. Campanella would have been present. But Lincoln is one of only two counties where residents of Washington State file uncontested divorces by mailing the paperwork to the county clerk. Neither petitioner has to be present, nor do they have to have legal representation." When she noticed his skeptical expression, the tension headache she'd been fighting began to pound unmercifully. "It's really quite simple. The judge looks over the papers, signs a final judgment and sends it back."

"That sounds out of character, for a lawyer

to pass up a case like this," Blake said, frowning. "Most of the ones I know would jump at the chance to make some easy money."

"Mr. Campanella is the grandfather of one of my coworkers," she explained. Karly really appreciated the woman's offer of help. When she'd come back from Vegas and realized the enormity of what she'd done, she'd been in a panic to fix her mistake. "Jo Ellen asked him to guide me through it all and he agreed. He suggested that I use the courts in Lincoln County since ours was a simple, uncontested divorce. He said it would save time and cost a lot less than going through the court system in Seattle. I agreed, and followed his instructions."

Blake nodded. "I guess that makes sense if you're in a hurry to rid yourself of an unwanted husband."

His words were bitter and cut like a knife. She had to swallow around the lump forming in her throat. He had no idea how hard it had been to make the decision not to follow her heart and move to the middle of nowhere with him. She had witnessed the unhappiness and resentment created when her mother followed her heart and it had ultimately ended her parents' marriage. Karly had reasoned that it was better to end things before it came to such hard feelings between herself and Blake. But there was no sense in dwelling on the mistakes and heartaches of the past now.

"I never said I was in a hurry to get rid of you."

He stared at her for a moment before he shrugged. "That's debatable, but it's not the issue. I need a notarized copy of the final decree."

Karly nibbled on her lower lip as she nervously met Blake's fathomless brown eyes. The time had come to lay out the reason for her visit and apologize for making such a mess of everything. "Actually, I don't even have a copy of it myself."

"Didn't they send you one?" he asked, his frown turning to a scowl.

"No, but I'm sure they will," she said evasively. She needed to explain what happened before she told him the reason she'd traveled all the way to Wyoming. "The import company I work for sent me to their offices in Hong Kong for several months shortly before the ninety-day cooling-off period was up and I wasn't able to check on it from overseas." Her head pounded as she thought about how badly she'd handled something as important to both herself and Blake as their divorce. But she'd been sad and unsure as to why she'd felt so badly about a logical, sensible decision that should have brought only relief. "When I got back last week, I called to inquire about our copies of the final decree."

He must have been able to sense that there was more to the story because Blake's scowl darkened. "What did they say?"

Shaking her head, Karly took a deep fortifying breath in order to tell him the rest of what had happened. "I called the Lincoln County courthouse to see if I could get a copy of the final decree…"

When she let her voice trail off as she searched for the right words, he prompted, "Yeah, I got that. You called about the papers. And?"

Karly briefly closed her eyes as she tried to gather her courage for what needed to be said. Opening them to meet his suspicious gaze, she did her best to keep her voice steady. "Apparently the papers were lost in the mail because the court clerk has no record of us ever filing for a divorce." She had to take a deep breath before she could finish. "It appears that we're still husband and wife, Blake."

"We're still married," he repeated as if he had a hard time grasping what she'd said.

"Yes." She hurried on as she reached into her purse to take out a new set of divorce papers. Her hand trembled slightly as she placed the envelope on the desk in front of him. "I'm really sorry for the inconvenience. Once you sign these, I'm going to fly to Spokane and drive over to the Lincoln County courthouse to file them with the clerk myself."

"So all this time, I've been thinking I'm a free man and I wasn't," he said, sitting back in the desk chair.

"Have you met someone?" she asked before she could stop herself.

He raised one dark eyebrow as he stared at her. "Would it matter if I had, Karly?"

Yes! "No," she lied. Thinking quickly, she added, "I was, um, afraid this snag might have derailed plans you might have made with someone else."

He continued to stare at her for a few moments before he smiled, shook his head and opened the envelope to remove the document. Reaching for an ink pen, he signed where she had flagged the papers with colored sticky notes.

"Well, you're stuck with me for at least another ninety days," he said, sliding the pages back into the envelope and pushing it across the desk's shiny surface toward her.

Karly winced at his acidic tone. She knew he was disillusioned and extremely unhappy with the situation. "I'm really…sorry, Blake. I never meant for any of this to happen." At least, not the mishandling of their divorce.

"Yeah, well, it did," he said, sounding resigned. "When you file these at the courthouse, make sure they send me copies of everything."

"Of course," she said, nodding as she slid the envelope back into her shoulder bag. She hesitated a moment as she tried to think of some way to say goodbye. Deciding there wasn't anything she could say that wouldn't make matters worse, she rose to her feet. "I'll be in touch if there's anything else we need to do."

"Did you drive all the way from Seattle or is that little toy in the driveway a rental?" he asked, standing up.

"I rented it when I flew into the Cheyenne Regional Airport," she answered, wondering why he wanted to know.

"I'll check under the car before you leave to make sure you didn't do some kind of damage to the undercarriage," he said, taking his wide-brimmed hat from the hook as they left the room. "You hit quite a few potholes on your way up the lane. Drive slower on the way back. You'll be less likely to damage the car."

"Who's responsible for taking care of the roads around here?" she asked. "They're in terrible condition."

"The county is responsible for the roads leading up to the ranch property lines, but ranchers have to keep the roads on their land plowed in the winter and graded in the summer," he explained. "We took care of grading the road after the snow melted off in the spring. But once the rainy season hit it washed out a lot of places. We were waiting until it dried up to work on the road again, when we have time."

"I think it's safe to say it's dry enough," she said as they walked out of the house. She didn't know much about caring for a ranch or tending to roads, but she did notice the red sports car was coated with a thick layer of Wyoming dust.

His deep laughter sent heat racing through her veins and reminded her of the carefree man she'd met eight months ago. The man he'd been before she'd told him she couldn't be his wife after all. "It won't be an issue much longer," he stated. "The new owner is having it asphalted all the way to the county road."

"Why didn't the previous owner do that?"

she asked, walking across the yard with him to the rental car.

"After her husband died, she wasn't interested in anything but trying to sell the ranch to a land developer. When she tried for a couple of years and failed to find a buyer, she finally sold it to one of her husband's sons from a previous marriage," he answered, sounding a little angry as he kneeled down to peer under the car.

She briefly wondered why he would be upset by a property dispute between the owner's heirs, but she abandoned her speculation when her cell phone chirped. Taking it out of her shoulder bag, Karly looked to see who was texting her. Her heart sank as she read the message. It was an alert from the airline, informing her that due to a contract-workers strike at the Denver airport, all flights had been canceled until further notice. Since the only commercial airline going in or out of the Cheyenne airfield was from Denver, she wasn't going anywhere until the labor dispute was settled.

"Lovely," she muttered sarcastically. Now what was she supposed to do?

She'd packed light because she hadn't expected to be away from home for more than a couple of nights. And she certainly hadn't planned on having to find a local place to stay indefinitely while the strike was settled.

"Looks like everything is intact," Blake said, unaware of her dilemma. He straightened to his full height as he dusted off his hands. "When does your flight leave?"

"It's not leaving," she said disgustedly as she opened the browser on her phone to see what lodging was available in the nearest town. "All flights in and out of Denver have been canceled due to an airport workers' strike."

He remained silent for several long moments and when she looked up, he was staring at her. "Looks like you'll be spending some time on the Wolf Creek Ranch after all," he said, folding his arms across his wide chest.

"No, I'll get a room in town," she said determinedly. It had been hard enough to see him again, to sit across the desk from him. She couldn't imagine spending the night in the same house with him, knowing he was so close and not being able to touch him or have him hold her.

He pointed toward the mountains to the west. "Not tonight you won't. I can't, in good conscience, let you drive on unfamiliar mountain roads in the dark. Hell, it would be a miracle if you didn't get lost or end up hung in the top of a tree after missing a curve and going over the side of the mountain."

"You *can't allow* me to drive back in the dark?" she demanded indignantly. "I have news for you, buster. If I choose to go, you aren't going to stop me."

He closed his eyes and shook his head as if trying to gather his patience. When he opened them, he looked directly at her. "I realize we won't be married for much longer, but right now, I'm still your husband," he finally said. "I take my vows seriously. It's my job to keep you safe until a judge says otherwise. I'd feel a lot better if you would at least wait to make the drive until tomorrow morning. It's safer."

Karly was surprised by his grudging admission that he thought he should protect her. There hadn't been anyone who'd cared about her safety since her mother passed away several years ago. But as nice as it was to have someone worry about her well-being again, she needed to remember that Blake was only doing it because he felt it was his obligation. He'd signed the divorce papers. He must be as ready to undo their mistake as she was.

Sighing heavily, she tried to decide what to do. Everything about this trip had gone awry. Her flight from Denver to Cheyenne had been delayed for over two hours due to a dangerous storm front moving through, the drive to the ranch had taken three times as long as she had anticipated due to the car the rental agency had provided and her meeting with Blake hadn't gone as quickly as she'd thought it would. The way her luck had been running, it was very likely that she'd end up in one of the disastrous scenarios he mentioned.

"Eagle Fork is only twenty miles away," she said, glancing at the sun rapidly sinking behind the mountains to the west.

"It takes a little over an hour in the daylight to drive down the mountain to get there. How long do you think it would take you to get back at night?" Blake pointed toward the road. "Do you really want to drive on unfamiliar, rough mountain roads in the dark? At least stay tonight."

"If I take it slow, I shouldn't have a problem," she hedged. Sleeping in the same house with Blake—even if it was in different rooms— wasn't a good idea. He was six feet two inches of male temptation that had proved almost impossible for her to resist in the past. It had taken going all the way back to Seattle for her to realize the effect he'd had on her good sense. What crazy decisions would she make if she stayed here with him?

"And what happens if you have a deer or elk run across the road in front of you?" he persisted, oblivious to her inner battle. "I've got news for you, sweetheart. If you hit one of those in that little toy car, you're going to lose."

Karly stared at him as she weighed her options. Driving up through the mountains during the day with all the switchbacks and ninety-degree curves had been a challenge. And of course, there had been the last several miles to the ranch, which had become a dirt-and-gravel road pitted with more holes than a piece of Swiss cheese. But at night?

She hated to admit it, but her choices were extremely limited. Since she didn't know another soul in Wyoming, she either had to risk going down the mountain in the dark to find a motel room in Eagle Fork, or stay with Blake.

As she watched the evening shadows begin to overtake the high mountain valley, she decided she had run out of time. There simply wasn't enough daylight left to make it back to town before it got completely dark.

"I suppose I could spend the night here and then drive back down to Eagle Fork tomorrow to get a room for however long it takes the strike to be resolved," she said, talking more to herself than to Blake.

"Then it's settled," he said, walking to the back of the car. "I'll carry your luggage inside."

"I wasn't expecting to spend more than two nights away from home and only have an overnight case," she said, using the keyless remote to open the trunk as she walked over to take the small bag from him. "I can bring it inside."

He shook his head as he lifted it from the trunk. "Grandma Jean would have my hide if she got wind of me letting you carry your luggage yourself."

"Does she live close by?" Karly had never known what it was like to be close to a grandparent. Three of hers had passed away before she was born and her paternal grandmother had lived so far away, she'd only seen her a handful of times.

"She lives down in Eagle Fork," he said as he placed his hand at the small of her back to guide her into the house. "There were several of us who lived with her during the winter when we were still in school."

"Because of all the snow?" she mused as they climbed the stairs to the second floor. If the roads were so difficult to navigate in the summer, she couldn't imagine trying to get around in a heavy snowfall.

"It was easier to stay down there where we could get to school than have to miss and make up all of the schoolwork when we were finally able to get back to class," he said, nodding as he stepped back so she could enter a bedroom. When he set her small suitcase on the bed, he hooked his thumb over his shoulder toward the door. "While you get settled, I have to drive over to the main house to see about a few things the owner needs me to take care of."

"Was that the huge log home I passed just before I got here?" she asked, unzipping the overnight case to remove her flip-flops. She loved wearing heels, but she had been in them all day and her feet were beginning to hurt.

Blake nodded. "The owner had that built a couple of years ago. Right after he bought the ranch."

"It's beautiful," she said, removing the heels to put on the flip-flops. "And it's perfect for the rugged surroundings."

He stared at her a moment before he turned and walked out into the hall. "I guess I'd better go on over to the main house. Make yourself at home. I won't be long."

As she heard him descend the stairs, she

began to realize just how little she knew about the man she had married. In Las Vegas, Blake had literally swept her off her feet and charmed her into a fairy-tale week of romance, love-making and a wedding. But as idyllic as their time together had been, they hadn't talked about their families or jobs, their hopes or their dreams.

"It would have never worked between us," she murmured as she sat down on the side of the bed.

The realization was not a new one. So Karly had no idea why the words made her feel so sad. This was what she'd chosen—the way it had to be. She wasn't about to make the same mistakes her mother had made. She wasn't going to give up everything—her home, her lifestyle, her job—for a man and then resent him for her choices.

No matter how beautiful it was here or how cherished and safe Blake made her feel when he took her in his arms, she couldn't live on this ranch with him any more than he could live with her in Seattle. And the sooner she accepted that truth, the better off she would be.

Two

Blake glanced over at his backpack, the thermal food carrier and the jug of iced tea on the truck seat beside him as he drove away from the main ranch house. *His* house.

He had never lied to Karly, not eight months ago and not today.

But he hadn't been completely honest with her, either.

When they met in Las Vegas, he'd told her that besides competing in rodeo, he was the boss at the Wolf Creek Ranch in Wyoming. She had assumed that meant he was the foreman and he hadn't bothered to set her straight.

For one thing, they'd been so hot for each other, they hadn't talked at length about their jobs or much of anything else. And for another, he didn't go around flaunting the fact that he owned the Wolf Creek or that he was a multi-millionaire.

He had firsthand knowledge of how the lure of money could influence people and he intended to avoid that kind of shallowness at all costs. He didn't want the money to affect his relationships, and he'd been especially careful about what he'd shared with the woman he'd married so quickly. In the past, both he and his father had seen the ugly side of women hell-bent on getting their hands on a hefty bank-roll and once had been enough to leave Blake more than a little cautious.

But he was fairly certain Karly had no knowledge about the size of his bank account. She had fallen for him—without the influence of his money. He had figured that when she joined him at the ranch it would be a nice sur-prise to let her know that they would never have financial worries like a lot of other cou-ples starting out. Unfortunately, he hadn't had the chance to tell her the truth because she'd decided that living in a big city without him was preferable to living on the ranch with him.

She'd made that decision without the influence of his money, too.

In hindsight, he wished he'd told her right after they got married in Vegas. He didn't want her thinking that he had been trying to hide his assets because of their pending divorce. That wasn't the case at all. And he had every intention of telling her the truth, as well as providing her with a nice settlement for the very brief time they'd been married. He just needed to figure out the right time and way to go about doing that.

He could have told her about his wealth when she called from Seattle to tell him she thought they'd made a mistake and that ending the marriage would be for the best. But he'd decided against that because she might have assumed it was a desperate attempt on his part to get her to reconsider their divorce, to give them a chance. Him begging for a second chance was something that would never happen. Even if his pride had allowed it, it probably wouldn't have made a difference. She'd had her mind made up and nothing he could have said would have changed it.

So he'd kept his secret and signed the papers. But he could have told her the truth today, too, when she'd mistakenly assumed the foreman's cottage was his house and that the main house and ranch belonged to someone else. But he'd held back without really knowing why.

All he knew was that his ego had taken enough of a hit eight months ago, when he'd learned that while she might have been the woman of his dreams, he obviously hadn't been the man of hers. And if he was perfectly honest with himself, there had probably been a little fear holding him back, as well. He hadn't wanted to tell her he was rich and end up finding out that he'd been wrong about her—that Karly could be swayed by the temptation of his money.

As he steered his truck up the lane leading to the foreman's cottage, he reached up to rub the tension building at the back of his neck. He wasn't sure how something that had originally felt so right had gone so wrong. When he'd married Karly after only knowing her a week, the decision had seemed as natural as taking his next breath. Their whirlwind wedding carried on the Hartwell family tradition. Blake's Grandma and Grandpa Hartwell had been married three days after meeting and his father and mother tied the knot two weeks after their first date. Both couples had successful marriages until death separated them and

Blake had been sure it would be that way with himself and Karly. It was obvious now that he had been wrong.

Parking his truck beside the little red sports car, Blake took a deep breath and reached for his backpack, the thermal carrier full of food and the gallon thermos of iced tea he'd had his cook pack for their supper. There was no sense in trying to figure out how he could have misjudged Karly's commitment to their relationship. He had and there wasn't anything he could do about it now. Besides, he'd never been one to dwell on his mistakes.

As he walked toward the cottage, she opened the door and stepped out onto the porch. His breath caught and his heart thumped against his ribs. He felt the same pull that had drawn him to her the first time he'd laid eyes on her in Vegas. He forced himself to ignore the feeling. She might be the most exciting woman he'd ever known, but the sting of her rejection and her disdain for his lifestyle told him in no uncertain terms just how unimportant he was to her. She'd walked away from him once. He wouldn't give her another chance to do it again.

Distracted by his turbulent thoughts, it took him a moment to notice the frown on her pretty face. "Is something wrong?" he asked as he climbed the steps.

"Where do you keep your food?" she answered his question with one of her own as they entered the house. "I was going to make something for dinner, but the refrigerator and pantry are both empty. If you live here why isn't there anything in the house to eat?"

"I usually eat down at the bunkhouse with the single men or over at the main house," he said truthfully as he set the cooler and jug of iced tea on the kitchen island, then turned to hang his hat on a peg by the door. He did eat with his men at the bunkhouse occasionally, just not as often as he ate what his cook made for him in the main house.

She looked doubtful. "Even in the winter when you're snowed in?"

He couldn't help but laugh at her erroneous assumption. "Sweetheart, there's no such thing as getting snowed in around here. A ranch is a twenty-four-hours, seven-days-a-week operation. It never shuts down because the livestock are depending on us to take care of them. If it rains we get wet. If it snows we wade through it no matter how deep it gets or how cold it is."

"I hadn't thought of that." Looking a little sheepish, she shook her head. "I'll be the first to admit I don't know anything about ranching."

"Don't worry about it." He motioned toward the thermal carrier. "And don't worry about cooking. I had the cook over at the main house pack up what he made for supper. Why don't you set the table while I go wash up?"

He didn't mention that he'd had to endure an interrogation and a stern lecture before old Silas finished loading the carrier with containers of food. A retired cowboy turned cook after his arthritis prevented him from doing ranch work, Silas Burrows had some definite ideas on how Blake should conduct his life and he didn't mind sharing them every chance he got. Having a wife show up unexpectedly, one that Blake hadn't told Silas about, definitely got the old boy started. As sure as the grass was green, Blake knew he hadn't heard the end of what Silas had to say on the matter, either.

"I'll have dinner on the table by the time you return," she said as she started removing the food from the carrier to set it on the butcher-block island.

Blake watched her for a moment before he gritted his teeth and left the room. Karly had changed into a pair of khaki camp shorts and an oversize T-shirt while he was gone. She shouldn't have looked the least bit appealing. But he'd be damned if just seeing her in the baggy shorts, shapeless shirt and bright pink flip-flops didn't have him feeling as restless as a range-raised colt.

Disgusted with himself, he marched up the stairs and down the hall to the master bedroom. How could he want a woman who had rejected him? Who had rejected his way of life and the land he loved?

Setting his backpack on the cedar chest at the end of the bed, he walked into the adjoining bathroom to wash up. As he splashed cold water on his face to clear his head, he couldn't help but think about the irony of the situation.

When Karly called him a few days after they parted in Vegas to tell him that she had changed her mind about being his wife, she hadn't even been willing to discuss coming to Wyoming in order to see if they could save their brief marriage. Yet almost nine months later, here she was—in the very place she said she never wanted to see—with papers to end the union.

But as he dried his face and hands with one of the fluffy towels from the linen cabinet, he couldn't help but think there had to have been something that happened when she got back to Seattle that had caused her change of heart. But what could it have been? Was there someone else she hadn't told him about? Maybe an old flame or someone she had been seeing before they met?

He'd asked himself the same questions a hundred times—and just as often told himself to forget about solving the mystery. He had no way of knowing what went through her head. And no reason to ask once she'd been determined to end things between them.

But now that Karly was here, he had a golden opportunity that was just too damn good to pass up. All he had to do was convince her to stay at the ranch a few days, until the strike in Denver was settled. That would give him time to ask her what had happened, to find out what had changed her mind and why.

It might not be the smartest thing he'd ever wanted to do. And he knew that whatever he found out wouldn't change the state of their marriage; he'd already signed the papers and let her go. Hell, he'd probably be better off not knowing. And he certainly wasn't expecting anything about him or his ranch to change her mind, even if he did learn the answer.

But some perverse part of him felt that it

was his right to know why she'd refused to even try to make a go of things with him.

With his mind made up, Blake went back downstairs to the kitchen to help Karly set the table. "I've been thinking. It doesn't make any sense for you to spend money on a motel room when you can stay here for free," he pointed out as he got two glasses down from one of the cabinets.

"I can't do that," she said, looking at him like he had sprouted another head.

"Why not?" he asked, pouring them each a glass of iced tea from the thermal jug.

"I don't want to impose," she said, placing a container of country-fried steaks on the table.

"How would you staying here be an imposition?" He carried the glasses to the table, then held her chair for her to sit down. "We're still married and the last time I heard, a husband and wife staying in the same house isn't all that unusual," he added, laughing.

"We're not going to be married that much longer," she insisted. "We're practically divorced already."

"It doesn't matter." He shrugged as he seated himself at the head of the table and reached for the container of steaks. "You're still my wife and that gives you the right to stay here."

"We really don't know each other," she said, taking a bite of a seasoned potato wedge.

"That didn't seem to be a deal breaker when you said 'I do,'" he pointed out, before he could stop himself. He felt like a prize ass when he saw the wounded expression on her pretty face.

She stared at him for several long moments before she shook her head. "I think it would be best if I get that motel room tomorrow as planned."

"Look, I'm sorry about what I just said." He took a deep breath. "That was out of line."

She stared at him for a moment longer before she shook her head again. "Not entirely. We were both—" she paused, as if searching for the right words "—caught up in the moment in Las Vegas. And I don't think one of us was more at fault than the other."

Maybe she had been caught up in the moment, but he had known exactly what he was doing and the commitment he was making when he vowed to take care of her for the rest of their lives. But arguing that point wasn't going to accomplish what he had set out to do.

"That's all water under the bridge now," he said, shrugging. "But if you stay here, I'm sure you'll be more comfortable than in a motel room. And you won't have to drive the mountain roads more than once to get back to the airport."

She gave him a suspicious look. "Why are you being so persistent about this, Blake?"

"I figure it will save you a few hundred bucks or so," he said, thinking quickly. She obviously had to watch her finances. Otherwise, she wouldn't have mentioned that by filing the divorce herself instead of having a lawyer do it for her she was saving money. But he wasn't going to point out that he knew she was on a tight budget. She had her pride, the same as he did, and bringing up the state of her financial situation would probably send her back down the mountain as fast as that little red car could take her. "Besides, staying here beats sitting in a motel room for several days with nothing to do but stare at the four walls."

He almost groaned aloud when she nibbled on her lower lip as she mulled over what he'd said. She wasn't trying to be seductive, but it seemed like everything about her had his libido working overtime. Maybe it was due to the memories of making love to her that haunted his dreams at night. Or, more likely, it was the fact that he hadn't been with a woman since they'd parted ways in Las Vegas. Whatever the reason behind his overactive hormones, he had every intention of ignoring them.

"I suppose not having anything to do would be pretty boring," she finally conceded. "But I wouldn't have anything to do here, either."

"Sure you would," he said, careful not to sound too eager. "There's never a lack of things to do around a ranch. You could help me feed the horses and a couple of orphaned calves. And tomorrow afternoon, you can ride up to the summer pasture with me to check on a herd of steers we'll be moving back down here in a couple of weeks."

"You mean ride a horse?" When he nodded, she vigorously shook her head. "That's not an option."

"Why?"

"Other than a pony ride at the grand opening of a grocery store when I was five, I've never been on a horse," she said, taking a sip of her iced tea.

That explained her skittish reaction to Boomer when she'd first arrived. "Don't worry about it. I've got the perfect horse for you and it won't take any time to teach you how to ride her."

"I don't think that would be a good idea,"

she commented, reaching for a roll. "Horses don't like me."

"Why do you say that?" he asked. "You just admitted that you've never really been around horses. How would you know if they like you or not?"

She frowned. "Your horse snorted and stomped his foot at me this afternoon. If that wasn't an indication he didn't like me, I don't know what is."

"Hoof," he countered, correcting her. "Horses have hooves and he was just shooing away a fly when he moved his leg." Blake took a bite of his steak. "And for the record, Boomer didn't snort. Gently blowing through his nose like that is a horse's way of sighing. It signals that he's relaxed, curious or in some cases just saying hello. Boomer was just being friendly."

"His name doesn't exactly instill a lot of confidence," she said, shaking her head. "Boomer sounds rather...explosive."

Blake laughed out loud at her inaccurate assumption that the gentle gelding's name reflected his temperament. "Boomer is short for Boomerang and the reason he got that name is because he likes people so much he can't stay away from them. I can turn him out into a pasture with other horses and before I know it, he turns around and comes right back to me."

"That's great, but it doesn't mean he likes *me*," she said, looking doubtful.

Blake grinned. "I'll introduce you tomorrow morning when we go out to the barn to take care of the calves. You'll see. He's as gentle as a lapdog."

She looked skeptical, but didn't comment until they had finished their meal. "I can help you feed the babies, but I'm afraid riding a horse tomorrow is out of the question. I didn't expect to be away from home more than a couple of nights and I really don't have anything to wear that would be suitable for a horseback ride."

He smiled at the relief he heard in her soft voice. He'd bet every dime he had that she'd spent the entire meal trying to think of a way to get out of riding.

"We'll remedy that tomorrow morning after I get the feeding done," he said, smiling as he helped her clear the table. "We'll make a trip down to Eagle Fork's Western store and get everything you need."

"That sounds like a lot of time and trouble for a pair of jeans," she said as she put containers of leftovers into the refrigerator. "And besides, I don't want to interfere with the work you need to get done."

"It won't be any trouble at all," Blake said, barely able to keep from laughing at her attempts to escape his plans. He was not only determined to find out what she wasn't telling him, he was also going to give her a ranch experience she'd never forget. "I need to get a new shirt for a Labor Day barbecue on Monday anyway and you'll need something to wear to that as well. In fact, it would probably be a good idea to get you enough clothes for a few days since there's no telling how long the strike will last."

"I can't crash your friend's party," she said as she turned to wipe off the kitchen island.

"You won't be crashing the party." Blake wasn't about to take no for an answer. "You'll go as my date."

"That would be rather awkward," she insisted.

"Only if you make it that way," he said, even though he knew she was right.

"How on earth would you even introduce me?" She gave him a pointed look. "We may be married right now, but we're little more than strangers on the way to a divorce. We wouldn't even be married if the papers had arrived as they should have. I'd just as soon avoid a lot of questions about our hasty marriage and the upcoming divorce."

"Easy. I'll just tell them that we met in Vegas and you came for a visit," Blake explained.

She stared at him before she frowned. "Do you really think it will take that long for the strike to be settled?"

He shrugged. "It's a holiday weekend. There's really no telling. Even if they come to an agreement over the weekend it's going to take at least a day or two for the airlines to get all of the schedules lined up and the passengers from the canceled flights who haven't found other means of transportation on their way again. And with Labor Day on Monday that's going to delay things even more."

"I suppose I could drive from here to Lincoln County," Karly said, looking thoughtful.

"I know you want to get this divorce over with, but do you really want to drive fifteen or sixteen hours in holiday traffic?" he asked. "You couldn't possibly get there tomorrow before the courthouse closes and it won't reopen again until Tuesday. By that time the strike might be settled and you'd be able to fly."

She didn't look happy about what he was

saying, but she finally nodded. "You're probably right."

"I know I am." When she yawned, he
pointed toward the hall. "I can finish clean-
ing the kitchen. Why don't you go ahead and
turn in for the night? Mornings around here
start early."

"How early are we talking about?" she asked,
hiding another yawn with her delicate hand.

"I'll start feeding the livestock in the barns
around dawn," he said as he loaded the dishwasher. "That will take about an hour. Since
you don't really have suitable clothes for that
yet, I'll wake you up after I get finished."

She looked horrified. "Good Lord, are the
animals even awake at that time of day?"

"They're not only awake, they're usually
making a lot of noise because they know it's
time for breakfast," he said, laughing.

When she yawned again, she started toward
the hall. "In that case, I think I'll follow your
advice and go to bed." She stopped at the door
and turned back. "Thank you, Blake."

"What for?" he asked, walking over to her.

"For giving me a place to stay until the
strike is settled and for being so nice about
all of this," she said quietly. "You really didn't

have to be, considering how badly I handled filing for the divorce."

He barely resisted the urge to reach for her. As he stuffed his hands into the front pockets of his jeans to keep himself from doing something stupid like taking her in his arms and kissing her until they both gasped for air, he shook his head. "Don't be so hard on yourself. You had no control over what happened after you put the papers in the mail. And like I told you earlier, I'm old-fashioned. As long as we're married it's my job to provide you with a roof over your head and something to eat."

She stared at him for several long moments before she finally nodded. "Well, thank you anyway. Good night."

"Yeah, see you in the morning," he mumbled as he watched her walk down the hall to the stairs.

Taking a deep breath, he waited until he heard her close the door to her bedroom before he started the dishwasher and turned out the kitchen light. As he slowly climbed the stairs to his own guest room, he couldn't help but wonder how everything had become so damn complicated. Eight months ago, things had been simple. He'd found the woman he was going to spend the rest of his life with and she'd told him that he was the man she wanted to share hers with, too.

He had no idea what had changed from the time they left Vegas until she called him a few days later from Seattle to tell him she wasn't joining him at the ranch as planned. But one thing was sure—before she left this ranch to file for divorce and return to her life in the city, he had every intention of getting an explanation and settling the matter once and for all.

The following morning, as Karly sat on the passenger side of Blake's truck, she looked out over the side of the mountain. On her drive up the winding road the day before, she'd been so focused on getting Blake to sign the new set of divorce papers and returning to Cheyenne to make her connecting flight back to Denver that she hadn't taken the time to notice the scenery. Although the mountains surrounding Seattle were more lush—with tall, straight conifers, beds of ferns and thick moss carpeting the forest floor—the ruggedness of the Wyoming landscape was no less beautiful. The pine and aspen trees didn't seem to grow as thick as the forests of the Northwest, but the jagged, snow-capped peaks and vast valleys of thick prairie grass, with colorful late-summer wild-flowers, were utterly breathtaking.

"It's really beautiful here," she murmured aloud.

"Imagine that." Grinning as he steered the truck around a tight switchback, Blake added, "It's amazing how different things turn out to be from our preconceived notions, isn't it?"

When she'd called to tell him she'd changed her mind about the marriage, she'd said some things about the land he so obviously loved that she deeply regretted. In hindsight, she'd been trying to convince herself that living in a remote area of Wyoming was unsuitable for her. She'd been trying to create enough distance between them to make divorce the best option. But that didn't change the fact that he'd taken offense at her comments. She'd hurt him unintentionally.

"I guess I might have been a bit hasty in my assumption that the area had nothing to offer," she finally admitted. "But you have to understand. I've lived most of my life in a city, where everything I want or need is close by."

"I understand that," he said, nodding. "But it's not the backwoods, off-the-grid type of living you envisioned, is it?"

"No," she admitted. "But you helped to create that misconception."

"How do you figure that?" he asked, frowning.

"You said the ranch was in a remote location and I naturally assumed…" She paused when she realized that with the closest neighbors at least ten miles away at the bottom of the mountain and only one way to get to the ranch, it really could be considered isolated. "I guess I thought that you meant it was without some of the modern conveniences."

"Tell the truth," he said, laughing. "You thought that a trip to the bathroom in the middle of the night would involve a flashlight and a little shed with a half-moon carved into the door."

She laughed. "Well, not quite. But I didn't expect it to have a main ranch house that looks like a log mansion, or the house you live in to have such a cozy feel to it. I guess I was thinking it would be more rustic."

"You've been watching too many old Westerns on television," he said, steering the truck onto the main road as they reached the bottom of the mountain. "Living on a ranch is like living anywhere else. We have modern appliances, satellite TV and high-speed internet.

About the only difference is having to drive a few miles to get to a store instead of it being just down the street."

"Maybe I have been thinking it would be like the Old West," she admitted thoughtfully.

They fell silent for the rest of the drive and by the time they reached downtown Eagle Fork, Karly had come to a conclusion that she wasn't overly proud of. She wasn't going to tell Blake, but it wouldn't have mattered if the ranch was rustic and isolated or sat right in the middle of a town. Her choice to divorce him would have been the same. It wasn't the challenges of living on a ranch that had held her back. It had been the fear she would turn out to be like her mother and discover that a husband and family weren't enough for her—that her career was more important.

A few minutes later, when Blake parked his truck in front of the Blue Sage Western Emporium, Karly noticed that the store looked as if it had been in business since hitching posts were used instead of parking meters. Abandoning her disturbing thoughts, she focused on their shopping trip. She hoped the clothing wasn't going to be too expensive. She wasn't poor, but she did live on a budget and hadn't planned on buying clothes that she probably wouldn't wear past the few days she was stranded at the Wolf Creek Ranch.

Blake grinned as he opened the passenger door to help her out of the truck. "Are you ready to get your cowgirl on?"

"Whether I'm ready or not, it looks like I'm going to," she said, feeling breathless.

She was in real trouble if his smile alone was enough to take her breath away. But it was the feel of his hand pressed to the small of her back as he guided her into the store that caused her knees to wobble.

Stepping away from him, she took a deep breath and the rich scent of leather assailed her senses. It reminded her of the man at her side and sent a shiver of longing straight through her. It would definitely be in her best interest to forego the shopping and make plans to drive to Lincoln County.

But even as she thought it, she knew that probably wasn't going to happen.

"Pick out as many pairs as you think you'll need," he said, ushering her over to a wall with large cubbyholes filled with folded pairs of women's jeans. He pointed to a couple of racks holding T-shirts and blouses. "And don't forget to get some shirts and something special to wear to the barbecue."

Before she could tell him that she wouldn't be needing clothes because she was going to leave the next morning to drive back to Washington State, a middle-age woman walked over to them. "It's good to see you, Blake," she said, smiling. She shot a curious glance toward Karly, as if wondering who she was. "How are things going at the Wolf Creek?"

"I can't complain, Mary Ann," he answered. "The hay crop was good this year and we should have more than enough to make it through the winter."

"That's always a relief," she said, nodding. "Eli Laughlin was in the other day and said pretty much the same thing about the Rusty Spur."

While Blake and the woman discussed what was going on at some of the other ranches in the area, Karly gave up on the idea of driving back to file the divorce papers. For one thing, she wasn't all that fond of spending so many hours in the car. And for another, sitting in a hotel room for a couple of days with nothing to do while she waited for the courthouse to open wasn't her idea of a good time, either.

Just as Blake had said, she'd be better off waiting here and looking for a way home after the holiday weekend. Most likely the strike would be done, and the courthouse would definitely be open. She didn't want to consider why the decision to stay here, with Blake, made her feel so warm inside.

By the time she found jeans and a few shirts that weren't too pricey, Blake joined her. "Are you ready to try on boots?"

"I hadn't even thought about footwear," she said, wondering how long it would take for her budget to recover from all of her unplanned purchases. She glanced down at her feet. "I know I can't wear these heels and I don't suppose flip-flops are suitable for helping you feed the orphaned calves, are they?"

He shook his head as he led her toward the back of the store, where boxes of boots were stacked on shelves from the floor all the way to the ceiling. "Not unless you want to risk a nasty cut or broken toes when one of them steps on your foot."

"Not hardly," she said, deciding that a financial headache was preferable to physical pain. Since she'd decided to stay the long weekend at Blake's ranch, she supposed she had to go all in and as he so eloquently put it, "get her cowgirl on."

A half hour later as she and Blake walked out of the store, Karly frowned at all the bags and boxes he carried. She knew she couldn't really afford all the things she'd bought, but she hadn't expected Blake to pay for her shopping spree. This was probably another obligation for him, because he was her husband. And the only reason she'd said yes was because her bank account wouldn't let her reject his kind offer. But she seemed to be getting deeper into the role of a wife even though the whole point of this trip had been to finalize their divorce.

"You should have let me pay for all of this," Karly said. If he had, she would have definitely gone with fewer and more economical selections. "I doubt the owner of the ranch will be all that happy about you putting my clothes on his charge account."

"Don't worry about it. He doesn't mind me charging things on the ranch account. And, like I said, you're my wife. If you lived with me, you'd be charging things all the time." Grinning, he shrugged as he put the purchases onto the backseat of the club cab truck. "It's one of the perks of being the boss."

"There's a difference between charging one or two items and loading up the account." She pointed to the two boxes he added to the pile. "That hat was outrageously expensive and those boots alone cost more than I've ever paid for a pair of shoes in my entire life."

"A good hat and a comfortable pair of boots are worth whatever price you have to pay for them," he stated as he helped her up into the passenger seat.

"But I won't be here that long," she argued, trying to make him understand. "Something cheaper would have served the purpose just as well."

She'd tried to tell him when he insisted she put them on that they were far too expensive. But when he gently wrapped his hand around her calf as he took her high heel off to put one of the boots on, her brain had short-circuited. Somewhere between her vocal cords and opened mouth her objection had turn into a gasp of awareness. His smile and the twinkle in his sexy brown eyes indicated that he'd noticed, but he didn't comment as he worked the boot onto her foot and she couldn't get her voice to work long enough to protest further.

He closed the door, walked around the front of the truck and got in behind the steering wheel. "Let's get something straight. As long as you're at the ranch and we're still married, I provide for you. That includes the clothes and hat you'll wear and the boots on your feet.

There are some things that I won't skimp on, no matter how expensive they are, because in most cases, you get what you pay for. Hats and boots are two of those things." He surprised her when he reached over to cover her hand with his. "And don't worry about me charging all of this on the ranch account. When the bill comes in, I'll pay for it."

The feel of his calloused palm on her skin and the memory of how his hands had felt on her body when they made love sent a shiver of longing straight up her spine. She tried her best to dismiss the reaction as nothing more than nerves. But as they continued to stare at each other, she knew it was going to take everything in her to keep from falling under his charming spell again.

She quickly slid her hand from beneath his and concentrated on what he'd said. "Blake, I appreciate that you feel it's your responsibility to see that I have what I need," she said, choosing her words carefully. "But I don't feel right about you buying a whole wardrobe for me."

He gave her a cursory glance as he started the truck and steered it out of the parking lot onto the street. "Why not?"

"If I had handled the divorce differently, you wouldn't be in the awkward position of giving me a place to stay or feeling obligated to buy things for me," she said, feeling guilty. For that matter, if she hadn't been so impulsive and made promises she hadn't been able to keep when they were in Las Vegas, neither of them would have found themselves in their current situation.

"Don't beat yourself up over this," he said, surprising her. "You did what you thought was best and it didn't turn out the way you planned." He stared straight ahead as he added, "It happens to the best of us."

Her guilt increased when she realized he was talking about his own plans for them to live together as husband and wife. He had every right to be bitter about how she'd ended things, but instead he was treating her like the wife she'd never been to him. Suddenly, she was wishing things could have worked out differently—but she quickly squashed that traitorous thought. "I suppose you're right," she murmured.

They fell silent for several minutes as Blake drove out of town toward the ranch. "Why don't we start over?" he suggested, breaking the silence.

She frowned. "What do you mean?"

"There's no sense wasting time pointing fingers or feeling guilty about what went wrong between us," he said pragmatically. "We've both signed the papers already. So why don't we forget the real reason for your trip to the ranch and look at this holiday weekend as a friendly visit? I'll show you what ranch life is all about." He laughed. "And you can look on your time here as one of those vacations people take just to play cowboy."

Her chest tightened at his offer, at the consideration he was showing her. They both knew she was to blame for the entire fiasco and that he had been terribly disappointed with her decisions. But he was willing to put aside any hard feelings in order for her stay at the Wolf Creek Ranch to be more pleasant. If she hadn't been so afraid that quitting her job and moving so far away from the city would turn her into her mother, she would have loved having this man for her husband.

"Thank you, Blake," she said, blinking back tears. "I think I'd like that."

"Then it's settled." His grin caused her pulse to flutter. "Let's get back to the ranch so we can get started on giving you the ranching experience of your life."

Three

The lingering shadows of night were just giving way to the misty light of dawn when Karly followed Blake out of the house and across the ranch yard toward one of the barns. Wearing a new pair of jeans, a hot pink T-shirt, her hat and a flannel-lined denim jacket he had insisted on buying her the day before, she stepped around puddles left by the thunderstorm that had popped up yesterday afternoon to keep from getting her expensive new boots wet.

The rain had prevented her and Blake from riding up to check on the herd of cattle in the upper pasture when they returned from the store and that had been just fine with Karly. It had given her a day's reprieve from having to learn to ride a horse. It was probably too much to hope for that it would rain again today.

"How long does it take to feed the animals?" she asked when they entered the barn.

"It takes longer right now than it usually does because of the bucket babies," Blake answered, opening the door to a room filled with large sacks of grain and assorted sizes of buckets. "But we're usually finished in about an hour."

She assumed the bucket babies he was talking about were the orphaned calves. When he set two pails with large nipples protruding from the bottom edge on a small table outside of the door, she understood why he called them bucket babies.

"Why don't you use big bottles?" she asked. "Wouldn't that be easier?"

He laughed. "Two reasons. One, we'd be stopping to refill the bottle every few minutes. And two, calves tend to be extremely enthusiastic when they eat. Holding a bucket can be hard enough when they get going. But holding a bottle would be damn near impossible."

"How old are they?" she asked, when he

started scooping cream-colored powder into each bucket. "If they're still on baby formula, they must be quite young."

"They're almost four weeks old," he said, adding premeasured jugs of distilled water to the buckets. He handed her a smooth wooden paddle. "If you'll stir the formula, I'll measure up the grain starter."

"They're already eating solids?" she asked, frowning. "Aren't they a little young for that?"

He laughed. "You know what they say. Kids grow up real fast these days."

She rolled her eyes. "Will you be serious? It was a legitimate question."

"Sorry," he said, continuing to chuckle.

"No, you're not." She couldn't help but laugh with him.

"Not really. I just couldn't resist." As he shook his head, his charming grin sent goose bumps shimmering over her skin. "Calves usually start nibbling on grass out in the field when they're a day or two old. But that's when they have their mamas with them and are able to nurse whenever they want. Because these calves are orphaned and have to be fed on a schedule, we start them on a little bit of hay a few days after they're born and grain starter about a week after that. When they're up to eating about a pound or two of grain a day we start weaning them away from the milk replacer. That's when they are about six to eight weeks old."

"They really do grow up fast," she said, marveling at how quickly the animal babies progressed.

While she stirred the calf formula, he went back into the feed room and began scooping grain into shallow pails. Glancing through the doorway to watch him, Karly decided that Blake Hartwell was without a doubt the most handsome, charismatic man she'd ever met. She was going to have to be extremely careful not to fall for him all over again.

That thought should have sent her speeding down the mountain as fast as the red sports car she'd rented could take her. But she had told him she would stay until the strike was settled and she'd already broken enough of her promises to him. She wasn't going to add another, especially after he'd been so nice about everything that had happened between them.

When he rejoined her in the wide barn aisle, he handed her the lighter pails with small amounts of grain starter in them and picked up the heavier buckets with the formula she had finished mixing. "Are you ready for your first lesson in the fine art of feeding calves?"

She nodded. "I guess I'm as ready as I'll ever be."

Other than the pony she'd ridden at the grocery store grand opening when she was in kindergarten, she'd never been around an animal larger than a cat or a dog and she was definitely feeling a little intimidated. Did calves have a tendency to bite? She didn't remember hearing of anyone suffering a cow bite. But that didn't mean anything. She knew absolutely nothing about livestock. And other than Blake, she didn't know anyone else who did.

That was another reason that she'd gotten cold feet about their marriage. She'd not only feared quitting her job and finding herself feeling as displaced and resentful as her mother, she would have also been living on this ranch with animals large enough to squash her like a bug.

The first time she'd ever seen those animals in action had been in Las Vegas when she met Blake and he'd invited her to watch him ride in the rodeo events. After returning to Seattle and remembering what the huge animals were capable of doing and the injuries their actions caused, she'd known for certain that ranch life wasn't for her. Yet, here she was doing the very thing that she'd feared—interacting with the beasts.

But when they reached the stall where the calves were, Karly couldn't help but smile. The two bucket babies immediately started bawling and pushing at the gate as she and Blake approached, as if they knew their breakfast had arrived.

"They're so cute!" she said, looking over the top board at the black calves. They seemed too little to do much damage. "Do they bite?"

Blake laughed as he set the two buckets of milk on a bale of hay outside of the stall, then took the pails of grain starter from her. "Cattle would have to have upper front teeth before they could do that."

"They don't have teeth?" she asked, doubtfully. She thought most all animals needed teeth to eat.

He shook his head. "They only have bottom incisors and a tough, thickly padded top gum, so it's highly unlikely that one could bite you and cause an injury. And even if they tried it, which they aren't prone to do, it would be more of a pinch than a bite."

"That's good to know," she said when he opened the stall door.

"I'll take care of feeding them the grain starter and then we'll give them the milk together," he said, entering the enclosure.

He was immediately accosted by the calves and she was amazed at how quickly the pair finished off the grain in the pails Blake held. "You were right about them being enthusiastic eaters," she said, laughing. They reminded her of two rather large, clumsy puppies.

When he walked out of the stall to get the buckets of calf formula, he chuckled. "Just wait until they see these. They'll be like sharks in a feeding frenzy."

Karly opened the door to the stall for him and cautiously followed him inside. The calves nudged up against her as they looked for the buckets Blake held. One of them even took two of her fingers in its mouth and started sucking.

"Oh, my." The calf hadn't hurt her and she laughed as she pulled back her hand. "They really are in a feeding frenzy."

Grinning, he nodded. "Just wait."

He showed her how to hold the bucket and she immediately understood what he meant. The calf she was feeding started butting its mouth against the bucket as it sucked on the nipple.

"Why is it doing that?" she asked, frowning.

"It's instinctive," he explained. "Out in the pasture, calves butt their mother's udder to help bring down the milk."

The calves had the buckets drained in no time and Karly couldn't help but wonder if they had to be on a four-hour schedule like human babies. "When will they need to eat again?"

"One of the other guys will feed them again in about twelve hours." He put a couple of flakes of hay in the stall, then washed the buckets and put them into plastic bags. When he finished, he smiled. "So what do you think of your first ranch experience?"

"I can't believe I'm going to say this, but I actually liked taking care of the orphaned calves," she admitted as they walked out of the barn. "They were so cute and when they looked up at me with those big brown eyes, I couldn't help but fall in love with them."

"If I remember correctly, you said something similar to me when we were in Las Vegas," he said, his voice low and intimate.

Karly swallowed hard as she gazed up at him. When they'd met, she had told him how much she loved his eyes. Gazing into the fathomless depths now, she found it hard to look away. Just as in Las Vegas, she felt as if she saw her future in the sexy warmth of his dark brown eyes and it took monumental effort to look away.

Blinking to break the spell, she gave herself a mental shake. That way of thinking was the exact reason she found herself in her current predicament and why she was facing the dissolution of their brief marriage instead of just ending a whirlwind affair.

Forcing herself to remember all the reasons why she had to stand firm in her decisions, she took a deep fortifying breath and attempted to change the subject. "Will my next ranch experience be breakfast?"

He stared at her for several long moments before he pointed toward the foreman's cottage. "While you go inside and wash up, I'll walk over to the bunkhouse and get something for us from the cook." Without another word, he turned and walked toward a building on the other side of the barn.

As she watched him go, Karly knew she should leave the ranch as soon as she could load the car. But she also knew she wasn't going to do that. For reasons she didn't want to think about, she felt compelled to stay with Blake until the strike was settled. Maybe it was due to the fact that she really didn't relish the idea of driving such a long distance. But more likely, it was the fact that every time she looked into his warm brown eyes she lost every ounce of sense she possessed.

Turning, she slowly walked to the house. Staying with him wasn't smart and she anticipated more than a few awkward moments over the course of the next several days. But with few other options open to her and a budget that couldn't really withstand a long stay in a hotel, she really didn't have much choice.

Now all she had to do was be strong and resist falling under his spell again. Unfortunately, that might prove to be a monumental challenge, considering that it only took a look from him for her to feel as if she would melt.

When Blake finished saddling the gentle buckskin mare, he glanced over at Karly, who was sitting on a bale of hay by the tack-room door. She looked about as nervous as a long-tailed cat in a room full of rocking chairs. All through breakfast, she had questioned him about riding a horse. She'd wanted to know what would happen in a number of situations— all of which were highly unlikely.

She'd looked so darned cute as she interrogated him about riding that it had been all he could do to keep his hands to himself. But as much as he'd like to take her in his arms and reacquaint himself with his wife's sweet taste, he resisted the temptation. Papers had been signed and it was just a matter of time before she went her way and he went his.

Besides, giving into his need for Karly wasn't going to get him any closer to finding out what had changed her mind about them. That's why he was going to do his best to ignore the fact that she still turned him on like no other woman ever had and concentrate on showing her the beauty of his ranch and the wonderful life they could have shared. In the bargain, he hoped to learn more about the woman he'd married and would soon let go.

"Karly, this is Suede," he said, forcing himself to smile as he led the mare over to where she sat. "She'll be your horse for as long as you're here at the ranch."

"She's awfully tall," Karly said, slowly rising to her feet. He noticed she was careful to keep him between herself and the gentle mare.

Trying not to laugh, he handed Karly the reins. "While you two get acquainted, I'm going to saddle Boomer."

"You're going to leave me alone with her?" she asked, sounding alarmed.

"Trust me, Karly," he said, trying to make

his tone as reassuring as possible. "If I thought there was even the slightest chance you would get hurt, I wouldn't let you get anywhere near this horse." Before he could stop himself, he reached out to cup her cheek with his palm. "I promise you'll be just fine, sweetheart."

As she continued to stare up at him, he felt the ever so slight sway of her body toward his. That was all it took to send his good intentions right out the window and before he could stop himself, he leaned forward to cover Karly's mouth with his. Soft and every bit as perfect as he remembered, her lips molded to his and when her mouth parted on a soft sigh, Blake's heart took off like a racehorse out of the starting gate. He couldn't have stopped himself from deepening the kiss if his life depended on it.

Tracing her lips with his tongue, he slipped inside to reacquaint himself with her silky inner recesses. Every one of his senses sharpened and his lower body came to full arousal faster than he thought was humanly possible. Her taste and the tiny moan that she couldn't quite stifle caused him to groan with frustration. They were in a barn holding a horse by the reins. Not exactly the ideal situation to start something he knew damn well he wouldn't finish anyway.

When he felt himself fighting the urge to pull her into his arms and kiss her until they were both utterly senseless, he dropped his hand and took a step back. "You trust me, don't you?"

Apparently as stunned by the intimate moment as he had been and just as reluctant to comment on that kiss, she stared at him for several long moments before she finally nodded. "Y-yes. But if you're wrong about me and this horse, I swear I'll come back and haunt you."

He laughed out loud as much to relieve the tension gripping him as at the humor of her threat. Her quick wit was one of the things that he'd found so damn attractive about her. And he took her humor now as a good sign; she was becoming more relaxed with him again.

"If you want to score points with Suede, scratch her forehead and talk to her," he said as he turned to go get Boomer out of his stall. When he returned, he was glad to see Karly had graduated to patting the mare's neck.

"I think we've come to an understanding," Karly announced as Blake saddled the gelding. "I'm not going to upset her."

When she paused, he smiled. "It sounds to me like you've worked things out."

Nodding, she added, "We're both going to blame you if I do make the mistake of doing something she finds offensive."

"Now, why doesn't that surprise me?" he asked, grinning as he led Boomer over to where she and the mare stood.

"Probably because you're the one insisting that I have to ride a horse," Karly retorted as he handed the gelding's reins for her to hold as well as the mare's.

"Wh-what are...you doing?" she asked, her voice filled with panic once again.

"Don't worry, Boomer is just as well behaved as Suede," he called over his shoulder as he entered the tack room to get a rifle. They didn't have a lot of trouble with predators, but it was always wise to take protection along on a ride just in case.

"Just remember—"

"I know," he interrupted, returning to where she and the horses stood. "If something happens it's all my fault and you're going to haunt me for the rest of my days." He couldn't help but chuckle as he slid the rifle into the tooled leather scabbard attached to Boomer's saddle, then took the reins from her to lead the horses out of the barn to the round pen. "I guess it's fortunate for all concerned that I'm a damn good teacher."

"It's nice that you're humble about it, as well," she said, grinning.

Tying Boomer's reins to the top rail of the round pen, Blake turned to face Karly. "No brag, sweetheart. It's just a fact." He nodded toward the mare. "Now let's get you up in the saddle so you can start learning how to ride."

Her apprehension was apparent when she put her boot in the stirrup. But her expression changed to relief when she shook her head and lowered her foot to the ground. "This isn't going to work."

"Why not?" he asked, wondering what excuse she was going to come up with this time.

"I can't possibly climb up into the saddle with my knee under my chin," she said, shaking her head. "I guess you'll have to ride up to the pasture alone."

"That's an easy fix," he said, moving to stand behind her. "While you pull yourself up by the saddle horn, I'll give you a boost."

The offer had been an innocent one, but when he placed his hand on her delightful bottom to help lift her, he felt like the world came to a screeching halt. The feel of her body nestled in his palm sent his hormones racing through his veins like the steel bearings in a pinball machine.

He quickly helped her up into the saddle, stepped back and took a deep breath. Had he lost what little sense he had left? He wasn't looking for anything more to come from her visit to the ranch than finding out what had changed in the few days after they parted in Las Vegas. He was still recovering from his first heartbreak. No way did he want to start something new with Karly. So, considering the effect she still had on him, he'd do well to keep any kind of physical contact between them to a minimum.

If he hadn't known that before, he sure as hell did after that kiss and that touch.

"Dear Lord, I'm a lot farther off the ground than I thought I'd be," Karly said, her voice a little shaky.

"A little taller than that pony at the grocery store opening?" Blake asked, thankful for the distraction from his wayward thoughts.

"That would be like comparing a two-story house to the Seattle Space Needle," she retorted.

He chuckled and handed her the reins, then, taking hold of the mare's bridle, he led the gentle animal through the round pen's gate. "Just relax and move with her," he instructed as he stroked the horse's tawny neck. He showed Karly how to rest her boots in the stirrups with the heels down and the toes pointed slightly outward. "And when you feel comfortable enough, loosen the death grip you have on the saddle horn."

She shook her head doubtfully. "That's easy for you to say. You have both feet firmly on the ground. You're not the one sitting up here looking down at how far you're going to fall."

Blake grinned as he started leading Suede around the perimeter of the round pen. "Do you honestly think I'd let you fall and not catch you?"

Karly nibbled on her lower lip, causing him to bite back a groan. "I believe you would try. But what if you couldn't react fast enough? Or I was too heavy for you to hold on to?"

He frowned as he glanced up at her. "Did you see anything slow about my reflexes when you watched me ride bulls in Vegas?"

"Well, no…but—"

"Then why do you think I'd miss doing something as important as catching you if you fell?" he asked. "And for the record, I've been tossing around bales of hay that weigh more than you do every day since I was fourteen or fifteen years old. The day you're too heavy for me to catch is the day they bury me."

"But what if—"

"You can't let all of the what-ifs in life hold you back, Karly," he interrupted. He let go of the mare's bridle and continued to walk beside her as they made another trip around the inside of the round pen. "If you don't take a chance once in a while, you're just marking time. You're not living."

It was something his grandfather had always told him and Blake firmly believed it was true. It was one of the reasons he'd been so quick to ask Karly to marry him. He'd known what he wanted and he'd made her his. It was also the reason behind him asking her to stay at the ranch while he tried to find out why she'd been hell-bent on divorcing him. He might not like what was behind her abrupt decision, but at least he'd know for sure why she'd decided he wasn't the one for her.

Karly stared at him for several long moments. They both knew he was talking about more than her riding a horse. But she didn't seem willing to talk about it and he wasn't going to press her on the issue just yet.

Smiling, she finally shrugged. "If I didn't

step out of my comfort zone once in a while, I wouldn't be on this horse now, would I?"

"And you're doing a great job of riding her on your own, too," he commented, holding up both hands to show her she was riding the mare independently.

"Oh, dear Lord!" From the look on Karly's pretty face, he knew she was a hair's breadth away from all-out panic.

"Don't freak out," he said calmly. "I haven't been leading Suede since the first trip around the pen and you've done just fine." When they reached the gate, he opened it and stepped out to untie Boomer while the mare continued to walk slowly around the inside of the pen.

"B-Blake?"

"I'm just going to get Boomer so I can ride beside you," he reassured her. Swinging up into the saddle, he guided the gelding into the pen and caught up with Karly and Suede as they made another trip around the inside. "There are a few more things I want to show you, then we'll be ready to leave the round pen and start the ride up to the pasture."

"Are you sure that's a good idea?" Karly asked. "I'd hate to have to spend eternity haunting you."

"I'll take my chances on that, sweetheart," he said, laughing.

As he showed her how to guide Suede by doing nothing more than touching the reins to either side of the mare's neck, he noticed that Karly began to relax. She sat looser in the saddle and actually started moving with the mare instead of remaining as stiff as a ramrod.

On the third trip around the inside of the circular fence, Blake nodded toward the open gate ahead. "It's time we take this show on the road."

Karly looked doubtful. "I really don't think—"

"Good idea," he said, grinning. "Don't think. Just do it."

When they rode the horses out of the round pen, he could tell by the tightening around her mouth that Karly was anything but confident. But he admired her willingness to give riding a try. He just wished she had shown that kind of consideration to giving their marriage a chance.

By the time she and Blake reached the pasture where the herd of steers had spent the summer, Karly was feeling a little more sure of herself. Suede had proved to be as docile as Blake had promised and once Karly relaxed in the saddle, riding the mare wasn't bad at all.

"Are these mountains part of the Rockies?"

she asked, gazing at the splendor of the high mountain meadow.

"Yup. The Laramie Mountain range is part of the eastern edge of the Rockies," he answered, stopping his horse to look at the black cattle on the other side of the river that wound through the valley.

When she looked over at him inspecting the animals, she realized that he'd been right not to give up his way of life to move to Seattle with her. Blake Hartwell wasn't a man who was meant to be a city dweller. She could tell he loved living on this ranch, loved watching over the animals in his care. He was as deliciously rugged as this beautiful land and she couldn't imagine him living anywhere else.

As she continued to admire the man who had swept her off her feet eight months ago, she spotted the butt of a gun attached to his saddle that she hadn't noticed before. A sudden thought had her looking cautiously at the tree line surrounding the vast clearing. "Are there grizzly bears in the region?"

Grinning, he shook his head. "Black bear, mountain lion and bobcat, but no grizzlies."

All three species were prominent in the mountains surrounding Seattle and normally black bears and bobcats weren't overly aggressive unless startled or if they were being protective of their young. Although she was extremely cautious when she was in an area where they were known to be, she wasn't as concerned by them as she was by the mention of mountain lions. They were an entirely different matter. They were more aggressive and so silent, one could be within a few feet and a person might never realize the animal was there until it pounced.

Blake must have realized she was worried about the predators that might be close by. "Don't worry, the big cats and bears in the area don't normally wander down from the higher elevations unless there's a drought or a shortage of the game they prey on."

"What keeps them from making these cattle their next meal?" Karly asked as she gazed at the herd of steers grazing on the thick prairie grasses.

"Unlike grizzlies, black bears are too opportunistic to bother with hunting larger game," he explained. "They'll eat whatever is available— roots, berries, bugs, carrion. They'll even eat garbage or whatever else they happen to find along the way."

Karly laughed as she nodded. "They really aren't very discerning when it comes to what they eat. Sometimes one will come down from the Cascade Mountains into one of the suburbs surrounding Seattle and everyone has to secure their trash cans. If they don't, they risk having the trash strewn all over their yards show up on the evening news as a warning to others to take precautions."

"Yeah, bears like an easy meal," he agreed. "But mountain lions are natural-born hunters. We do have a problem occasionally with one of them straying down here. If we see one or find tracks too close to the herds or ranch buildings, we try to call the Fish and Wildlife Service and they send one of the game wardens to deal with a nuisance cat."

"Do they kill the animal?" Even though the predators scared her outside the confines of a zoo, she hated that something might be killed because it had the misfortune to wander into the wrong place.

To her relief, he shook his head. "Not always. They first try to trap it for relocation to a more remote area. Exterminating the animal is a last resort unless it's known to be a threat to humans or livestock."

"Is that what the gun is for?" she asked, eyeing the hardwood stock sticking out of the leather holder. "For protection in case one of them becomes a threat to us?"

His expression changed to one of determination as he nodded. "It's always better to be safe than sorry. I told you I'd protect you no matter what and I meant it." He gave her a look that caused her insides to quiver. "I give you my word that as long as there's a breath left in my body, I won't let anything happen to you, Karly."

The intense promise in his dark brown eyes stole her breath and reminded her of the kiss they'd shared in the barn. Neither of them had seemed to want to acknowledge that the chemistry they'd discovered between them in Las Vegas was just as strong, if not stronger, than it had ever been. As she continued to gaze into the fathomless depths of his eyes, she'd never felt as safe and secure in her entire life as she felt at that moment.

They both remained silent for several more moments before they started across the pasture toward the trail that led back down to the ranch. There wasn't a doubt in her mind that he would do whatever it took to protect her from any and all dangers.

Her heart skipped a beat as she thought of how difficult it was becoming to keep him at arm's length. He'd acted just like the husband she'd always dreamed of, even though she'd presented him with divorce papers to end their union. And it was getting harder and harder to remember why it was the best for both of them to go through with the divorce.

She sighed when she glanced at him from the corner of her eye. He might be prepared to protect her from the four-legged predators that could hurt her. But who was going to protect her from the force of nature that was Blake Hartwell?

Four

"I told you riding isn't as hard as you thought it would be," Blake said, smiling as he helped Karly dismount the mare.

"I think I need to join a gym," she commented as she patted Suede's neck and moved away from the horse. Karly's wince and the way she walked told him that she'd spent too much time in the saddle for her first time riding.

His smile faded. He could have kicked himself for being an inconsiderate jerk. A new rider needed to condition their thigh and back muscles on shorter rides before they attempted long hours in the saddle. Otherwise they risked soreness much like what someone would expect after a strenuous workout. How could he have been so thoughtless?

He'd been so caught up in showing her the ranch and his way of life, he'd forgotten all about her being new to the experience of being on a horse. Now she was paying the price for his oversight.

"Why don't you go on up to the house and try to relax while I take care of the horses?" he suggested.

"I think I'll take you up on that offer," she said, nodding. She smiled. "I may be out of shape, but you're right about the riding. I can't believe I'm going to say this, but I actually enjoyed myself."

As he watched her turn and walk slowly toward the house, he knew what he would do if they were at the main house. He'd make sure she took a nice long soak in the hot tub, then give her a massage with a good soothing liniment. His body tightened at the thought of once again touching her satiny skin as he ran his hands over her thighs and back. Then he would turn her over and sink himself...

"You're one sorry son of a bitch, Hartwell," he muttered as he brushed down the horses.

Karly was hurting from his insistence that she ride a horse and his carelessness about the hours she spent in the saddle. They'd both signed divorce papers that she was eager to file. But all he could do was think about what a pleasure it would be to make love to her again. If that didn't make him a prize jerk, he didn't know what did.

Blake took a deep breath to relieve some of his building tension. She obviously didn't want him touching her that way and if he wanted to preserve what little sanity he had left, he shouldn't want that, either. But as long as he kept his hands to himself, he could drive her over to the ranch house for some time in the hot tub to ease her discomfort.

Of course, that would require introducing her to Silas. Blake wasn't worried about the old guy telling her that Blake was the owner of the Wolf Creek Ranch. He knew that if he asked Silas to keep that information to himself, the old man would take it to his grave before he told a soul. But introducing his soon-to-be ex-wife and then keeping secrets from her was going to add a lot of fuel to the fire of the many lectures Blake would have to endure before Silas found something else he felt compelled to preach about.

With his mind made up, Blake took the saddles and bridles to the tack room, brushed down the horses, then led them back to their stalls. Giving them generous scoops of oats and flakes of hay, he reached for the cell phone clipped to his belt as he left the barn.

"I'm bringing Karly over for supper," Blake said when the old man answered.

"So you decided I'm decent enough to meet your bride after all?" Silas queried, his tone filled with sarcasm. "What changed your mind, boy? Did you finally fess up and tell her you own this spread?"

"You ask a lot of questions," Blake complained.

"Well, I would never find anything out if I didn't," Silas retorted. "So did you tell her?"

"No."

"Tarnation, boy! Why not?" The old man grunted his disgust. "The way I see it, that little gal's got a right to know just who she's hitched up to."

"I told you, I don't want my net worth influencing her decisions," Blake said, irritated that they were having the same argument they'd had every time he'd talked to Silas since Karly arrived on the Wolf Creek.

"Not every woman is as money-grubbin' as

that heifer your daddy married or as connivin'
as that little tart that tried to rope you into
marryin' her by claimin' you were gonna be
a daddy," Silas insisted. "All this gal did was
take a trip down the aisle with you. And she
did it so fast she must not have cared if you had
millions or if you were flat broke."

Blake groaned at the mention of the fiasco
with the buckle bunny that had taken place several years ago. He didn't like thinking about
the hell he'd gone through proving that he
wasn't Sara Jane Benson's baby daddy. Just
the fact that he'd given the rodeo groupie a
reason to accuse him had been bad enough.
There were some women a man could have a
good time with and then there were the ones
that when they came toward him, a man would
do well to turn around and run like hell. Sara
Jane fell into the latter category.

But he'd been a little drunk that night and
pissed off over his stepmother's latest refusal
to sell him his family's ranch. He'd regretted
his lapse in judgment the following morning,
but he'd been fit to be tied when Sara Jane
showed up a month later claiming that he'd
made her pregnant. When he finally discovered that Sara Jane had lied—that there wasn't
a baby and never had been—he didn't think

he'd ever been more relieved in his entire life. After he confronted her, the woman had finally admitted it was all a ruse to try to get money from him after she discovered that he wasn't just a dust-covered rodeo rider. But aside from narrowly missing the trap she'd set, the incident had taught Blake a valuable lesson about letting anyone know that his family owned one of the largest private ranches in the state of Wyoming.

"She may have married me fast," Blake finally answered. "But she divorced me just as fast. I'll tell Karly when the time is right."

"When's that gonna be?" Silas persisted. "You know the longer you wait, the bigger the chance of somebody tellin' her for you."

"The chances of that happening are slim," Blake said confidently. "The men have been leaving before daylight to make sure the fences are ready for the herds when we bring them down from the summer pastures. And I know I can count on you not to say anything."

"It ain't my place to tell that little gal," Silas said, sounding affronted that Blake even mentioned the possibility. "But what are you gonna do when you take her over to the Rusty Spur for that barbecue day after tomorrow? What if one of the Laughlins says somethin' about it? What are you gonna do then?"

"I'm going to call Eli and fill him in before we go over there," Blake stated. "Neither Eli or Tori will say a word about it."

He'd given it some thought on his and Karly's ride back to the house and he knew he could trust his friends not to mention that Blake owned the ranch, or pass judgment on him for wanting to keep that fact from Karly. Eli Laughlin and his wife, Tori, had their own unorthodox tale of how they'd met and married, not to mention the obstacles due to secrets of Tori's past and Eli's trust issues that they'd had to work through.

Tired of arguing with the old cowboy, Blake decided it was time to bring the conversation to an end. "Go ahead and set the table. We'll be over in about fifteen minutes."

Ending the call before Silas could come up with more of his endless questions, Blake took a deep breath. He might be irritating as hell, but Silas was right. Karly had married him because she wanted to, not because she thought she could get something from him. And even though they were headed for a divorce, it was becoming more difficult to defend his stance on not telling her.

A sudden thought stopped him dead in his tracks. Could she have rejected him and their marriage because she thought just the opposite about him? When she got back to Seattle, had she decided that he didn't make enough money to support her and the kids he had hoped they would one day have?

Blake shook his head as he climbed the back steps and started into the house. Either way, he needed to find out what her reasoning had been for ending things with him. Once he knew that, he could put this marriage fiasco behind him. Until then, he'd simply wait and see what he could find out.

When Blake drove his truck up the asphalted driveway toward the huge log lodge, Karly caught her breath at the sheer size and beauty of it. "This is absolutely gorgeous," she said, falling in love with the way the home and the rugged landscape complemented each other so perfectly. No other style of house would have looked as natural with the vastness of the land surrounding it. "Can you imagine living in a place like this?"

"You like it?" he asked, staring straight ahead as he parked his truck in front of the porte cochere covering the entrance to the house. Made with the same huge logs as the main structure, it provided shelter from the weather as well as added to the grandeur of the home.

"Who wouldn't love this?" she asked, noticing a small waterfall cascading over boulders not far from the stacked stone steps. It emptied into a little pool by the bottom step and looked so natural that it took a moment for her to realize it was man-made. "Everything about it is perfect." She frowned. "But shouldn't we be going through the back entrance?"

"Why would we do that?" he asked, sounding confused.

"It's not like we're invited guests," she said, shaking her head. "The owner—"

"He isn't staying here right now and even if he was, he wouldn't care." He grinned as if finding something humorous about her question. "He's a pretty easygoing guy."

She had a hard time believing anyone would want an employee and his guest taking advantage of their good nature. "And you're sure he won't mind us just walking in like we own the place?"

He laughed and shook his head as he got out of the truck and walked around to help her down from the cab. "Take my word for it, sweetheart. He doesn't have any problem at all with us making ourselves at home while we're visiting the main house."

When he lifted her from the truck seat and set her on her feet, he kept his hands resting at her waist as he gazed into her eyes. Her breath caught and her pulse sped up. He was going to kiss her again and heaven help her, she wanted him to do just that.

Mesmerized by the heated light in his incredible brown eyes, she could only watch as he slowly began to lower his head. But just when she thought his lips would cover hers, he took a step back and smiled down at her. "Silas is expecting us."

Not entirely certain whether she was disappointed or relieved that he hadn't kissed her, she blinked. "Silas?"

He nodded. "I think I'd better warn you," he said as he put his arm around her and guided her toward the steps. "The housekeeper here is ornery, opinionated and downright disagreeable at times. But the old cuss has a heart of gold and if he thought you needed it, he'd give you the shirt off his back."

"Does he know…about us?" she asked hesitantly. She'd only told a couple of her friends at work about what had taken place on her Las

Vegas vacation. But he hadn't mentioned telling anyone.

Blake nodded. "Keeping anything from
Silas Burrows is damn near impossible. But
don't worry. He's won't say a word to you about
it, unless you bring it up."

She doubted that would happen, but she forgot all about her concerns or the housekeeper's
opinion when they reached the entrance doors.
Hand-carved images of black bears and pine
trees overlaid the glass and added to the ap-
peal of the lodge.

But when Blake opened the door and they
stepped into the foyer, Karly couldn't believe
the rustic beauty of the home. "This isn't just
a log home, it's a mansion," she said as they
walked into the great room.

With a vaulted ceiling and massive fireplace
made of river rock, the room had a surprisingly
cozy feel for such a large space. But when she
noticed the panoramic view of the mountains
through the wall of windows on the opposite
side of the room, it felt as if the room opened
up to the landscape beyond.

"Do you like it?" Blake asked.

She nodded in awe as she continued to look
around the room. Even the interior walls were
made of logs. "It's gorgeous."

"I'll give you the grand tour after supper," he said, smiling as if her approval pleased him.

"I'd like that." As an afterthought, she added, "As long as you don't think the owner would mind."

"Not at all." Blake's sexy grin sent a shiver up her spine. "Trust me, he'll be fine with it."

"Supper's ready and if you want it hot you two better get in here."

Turning, Karly spotted an older man who looked like every child's favorite jolly old elf. On the portly side, his thick hair and long, full beard were snow-white and although he wore jeans, his green suspenders and long-sleeved red shirt would have convinced young and old alike that he might very well be Santa Claus.

As they walked toward him, Blake made the introductions. "Karly, this is Silas Burrows."

"It's nice to meet you, Mr. Burrows," Karly said, extending her hand.

He stared at her for several moments before he gave her a wide grin as he shook her hand. "Just call me Silas or Si." He motioned for her and Blake to follow him. "I fixed beef stew and sourdough bread for supper. It ain't fancy, but it's hot and there's plenty of it."

"If it tastes half as good as it smells, I'm sure it's going to be delicious," she said when they entered the kitchen and the smell of baking bread and the rich aroma from the bubbling pot on the state-of-the-art range assailed her senses. "Is there anything I can do to help you finish getting it ready?"

Silas shook his head. "Not really much left to do. While I slice the bread, I'm gonna let Blake pour us all glasses of iced tea and we'll be ready to eat."

After Blake guided her over to the large oak table across the room and held her chair for her to sit down, he whispered close to her ear, "It looks like you've got a fan."

"What do you mean?" she asked, barely able to keep from shivering when his warm breath feathered over her sensitive skin.

"I haven't seen Silas grin this much since the former owner's second wife sold the ranch to his son," he said, nibbling a kiss along the column of her neck as if it was the most natural thing in the world for him to do.

Startled by his show of affection, her heart pounded against her ribs and she tried not to think about what it might mean as he crossed the kitchen to pour their drinks. To distract herself, she looked around. She loved to cook when she had the opportunity and someone to cook for. Unfortunately, that only happened a few times a year—usually when she and her coworkers had a potluck lunch at the office. But if she had a kitchen like this one, she might be tempted to cook more. All of the appliances were commercial grade and top-of-the-line. And she absolutely loved the spaciousness and convenience of the entire room's layout. Cooking, even if it was just for herself, would be a joy in a kitchen like this.

As the two men finished putting the food on the table, Karly suddenly realized just how hungry she was. She and Blake had had an early lunch before her riding lesson and trip to the upper pasture. Glancing at the digital display on the microwave, she was surprised to see that had been almost seven hours earlier.

When both men brought the food and iced tea to the table, Silas filled their plates with thick stew. Seating himself, he pointed to her plate with his fork. "You'd better eat up, gal. There's more where that come from." He grinned. "And I made a chocolate cake for dessert."

"I'll be sure to save room for a piece," Karly said, picking up her fork. "I love chocolate."

Smiling, Silas nodded. "Most women do."

"How would you know what women like?" Blake asked, frowning.

Silas grunted. "Just why do you think men give women chocolates on Valentine's Day, hotshot?"

"I don't ever remember you having a girlfriend," Blake said, sounding doubtful.

Silas shook his head. "Don't go thinkin' I didn't have my pick of the women in my day, boy. I used to be quite the lady's man about forty years back."

Karly couldn't help but laugh as she listened to the good-natured banter. It was like a game of verbal one-upmanship and she could tell the two men thought the world of each other. Blake treated Silas like a favorite uncle or beloved grandfather and it was clear the old gentleman cared just as much for him.

By the time the meal was over and Silas served them all slices of the chocolate cake, Karly couldn't remember the last time she'd laughed as much. "You two are hilarious. How long have you known each other?"

"I've known him and his brother since the day they were born," Silas said, taking a bite of cake.

"You have a brother?" Karly asked, turning to Blake. He hadn't mentioned having a sibling. But then they hadn't really talked about family, or much of anything in their lives, when they were in Las Vegas.

He nodded. "Sean's a couple of years older than me."

"Does he live close by?" she asked, wondering what it would be like to have someone who shared the same memories of family and growing up. Being an only child, she'd never experienced that and she couldn't help but feel that she'd missed out on something meaningful.

"Sean has a ranch about twenty miles to the north—on the other side of the mountain," he answered as he took their empty plates to the sink.

"That must have been nice, having someone to play with when you were little," she said, unable to keep from feeling wistful about it. "I always wanted a sister or brother, but I guess it wasn't meant to be."

While Silas loaded the dishwasher, Blake poured them each a cup of coffee and rejoined her at the table. "I take it you are an only child?"

"Back in December, we didn't get around to talking about family," she admitted, nodding.

He eyed her over the rim of his coffee cup for several long moments before he set it on the table and reached to cover her hand with his. "There were a lot of things we should have discussed, but didn't."

The feel of his warm calloused palm covering her hand made her feel heated all over and she found herself longing for the way things might have been between them. Before she could give in to that longing and do something she shouldn't, she pushed her chair back. "I… suppose I should help Silas with the dishes," she said, needing to put distance between her and Blake in order to regain her perspective.

She hadn't traveled all this way to rekindle what they'd shared in Vegas. She'd come to put an end to it once and for all. But unlike the certainty she'd felt in Seattle when she'd first made the decision, the thought of ending it after this lovely visit made her want to cry and she wasn't entirely certain why.

But when she started to rise from the chair, her thigh muscles were so stiff and sore, her legs threatened to fail her. "I shouldn't have sat that long," she said, slowly getting to her feet.

"That's another reason I wanted to bring you over here," he said, starting to lead her into the great room. "You'll feel better after some time in the hot tub."

Karly stopped to stare at him. "Blake, are

you out of your mind? I can't get in the hot tub."

He looked thoroughly confused. "Why not?"

"For one thing, I don't have anything to wear." She motioned toward the double glass doors leading from the great room to the stone patio beyond. "And for another, I know the owner of this place may be good-natured, but I'm sure he would draw the line at having someone he doesn't know taking a dip in his hot tub."

"Trust me, sweetheart, he won't care," Blake said, guiding her out of the house toward the in-ground pool and spa. "I have free rein here, which means you do, too. You can slip out of your clothes and soak for a while in the hot tub and no one will be the wiser."

"I'm not going to go skinny-dipping in a stranger's spa," she said, looking around as they walked outside. If the owner had a hot tub, she certainly couldn't find it.

The sun had already gone down and the lights around the stone patio and pool made it look as if they were standing on the edge of a tropical lagoon. At one end, a waterfall cascaded down a huge natural-looking rock formation into the pool. But when she looked closer, she realized that the hot tub was set behind the curtain of water, as if it was inside a hidden cave.

He pointed toward the waterfall. "It's completely private. And I promise it will help to soothe your aching muscles."

Relief from the stiffness in her thighs and lower back did sound like heaven. "The owner—"

"Won't mind at all," he interrupted. He grabbed a couple of bath sheets that were sitting on a lounge chair they passed on the way to the waterfall.

"Where did those come from?" she asked, beginning to realize he had this planned all along.

"I laid them out when we first got here," he answered, looking smug. "It was while you were surveying the kitchen."

"You had this planned when you invited me up here for dinner," she accused.

He nodded and grinned. "Now take your clothes off and hop in."

Five

When Karly continued to glare at him, Blake frowned. "What?"

"I'm not taking my clothes off in front of you," she said, stubbornly crossing her arms beneath her breasts.

He tried not to remember how perfectly those breasts fit in the palms of his hands or how responsive her nipples were when he teased them with the pads of his thumbs. Obviously, he hadn't considered the full effect of the temptation she'd present when he'd come up with this hot-tub idea.

"Why not?" he asked, grinning and putting

YOUR PARTICIPATION IS REQUESTED!

Dear Reader,

Since you are a lover of our books – we would like to get to know you!

Inside you will find a short Reader's Survey. Sharing your answers with us will help our editorial staff understand who you are and what activities you enjoy.

To thank you for your participation, we would like to send you 2 books and 2 gifts – **ABSOLUTELY FREE!**

Enjoy your gifts with our appreciation,

Pam Powers

SEE INSIDE FOR READER'S SURVEY

For Your Reading Pleasure...

We'll send you 2 books and 2 gifts
ABSOLUTELY FREE
just for completing our Reader's Survey!

YOURS FREE!

*We'll send you two fabulous surprise
gifts absolutely FREE, just for trying
our books!*

Visit us at:
www.ReaderService.com

YOUR READER'S SURVEY
"THANK YOU" FREE GIFTS INCLUDE:
▶ 2 FREE books
▶ 2 lovely surprise gifts

PLEASE FILL IN THE CIRCLES COMPLETELY TO RESPOND

1) What type of fiction books do you enjoy reading? (Check all that apply)
- ◯ Suspense/Thrillers ◯ Action/Adventure ◯ Modern-day Romances
- ◯ Historical Romance ◯ Humor ◯ Paranormal Romance

2) What attracted you most to the last fiction book you purchased on impulse?
- ◯ The Title ◯ The Cover ◯ The Author ◯ The Story

3) What is usually the greatest influencer when you <u>plan</u> to buy a book?
- ◯ Advertising ◯ Referral ◯ Book Review

4) How often do you access the internet?
- ◯ Daily ◯ Weekly ◯ Monthly ◯ Rarely or never.

5) How many NEW paperback fiction novels have you purchased in the past 3 months?
- ◯ 0 - 2 ◯ 3 - 6 ◯ 7 or more

YES! I have completed the Reader's Survey. Please send me the 2 FREE books and 2 FREE gifts (gifts are worth about $10) for which I qualify. I understand that I am under no obligation to purchase any books, as explained on the back of this card.

225/326 HDL GKET

FIRST NAME	LAST NAME

ADDRESS

APT.#	CITY

STATE/PROV.	ZIP/POSTAL CODE

do not cancel, about a month later we'll send you 6 additional books and bill you just $4.55 each in the U.S. or $5.24 each in Canada. That is a savings of at least 13% off the cover price. It's quite a bargain! Shipping and handling is just 50¢ per book in the U.S. and 75¢ per book in Canada. * You may cancel at any time, but if you choose to continue, every month we'll send you 6 more books, which you may either purchase at the discount price or return to us and cancel your subscription.
*Terms and prices subject to change without notice. Prices do not include applicable taxes. Sales tax applicable in N.Y. Canadian residents will be charged applicable taxes. Offer not valid in Quebec. Books received may not be as shown. All orders subject to approval. Credit or debit balances in a customer's account(s) may be offset by any other outstanding balance owed by or to the customer. Please allow 4 to 6 weeks for delivery. Offer available while quantities last.

BUSINESS REPLY MAIL

FIRST-CLASS MAIL   PERMIT NO. 717   BUFFALO, NY

POSTAGE WILL BE PAID BY ADDRESSEE

READER SERVICE
PO BOX 1867
BUFFALO NY 14240-9952

NO POSTAGE
NECESSARY
IF MAILED
IN THE
UNITED STATES

◄ If offer card is missing write to: Reader Service, P.O. Box 1867, Buffalo, NY 14240-1867 or visit www.ReaderService.com ◄

aside thoughts of her lovely breasts. "We did a lot more than just take our clothes off in Vegas and I don't remember either one of us having a problem with that."

If looks could kill, she would have dropped him right there where he stood. "That was different," she insisted.

He raised one eyebrow. "How do you figure?"

"We were married."

He shook his head. "Not at first we weren't. If you'll remember I ran into you in the hotel lobby in Vegas on Monday morning just as you were arriving to check in." He smiled. "And I made love to you for the first time that night. We didn't get married until the following Saturday night."

"That was a long time ago," she said softly.

"Not really." Reaching out, he cupped her soft cheek with his palm. "Sweetheart, we're still married and I'm still your husband until a judge says I'm not. There's no reason for you to feel shy with me."

Her expression softened a little, but she was apparently going to stand her ground. "We haven't been together in over eight months, Blake." She shook her head. "And in three months we'll be divorced."

There was a sadness in her eyes that he hadn't expected. Was she regretting her decision?

The notion that she might be having second thoughts caused a hitch in his breathing and he didn't want to consider why. But he immediately abandoned the likelihood that she had changed her mind again. Just because she might be sorry for what had—or more accurately hadn't—taken place after they left Las Vegas, didn't mean anything. In light of the choices she'd made and the way things had turned out, he had his own doubts that it would have worked out between them, as well.

Fighting to keep from lowering his head to kiss her slightly parted lips, Blake dropped his hand to his side. "Follow me. There's an entrance at the side of the waterfall. Going in that way will keep you from getting your hair wet." Once they entered the secluded area, he flipped a switch, turning off the underwater lights in the custom-made, sunken tub. "You can put your clothes over there to keep them dry," he said, motioning toward a lounge chair a couple of feet away. Turning his back to her, he added, "Let me know when I can turn around."

"I still can't believe your boss won't have a

problem with someone using his hot tub without permission," she said.

He started to tell her she was beginning to
sound like a parrot, but the words lodged somewhere between his vocal cords and open mouth
when he heard the rustle of clothing being removed a moment before her jeans and T-shirt
landed on the end of the lounge chair. Blake
swallowed hard. Then he took a deep breath
when her lacy panties and bra landed on top
of the pile. Just knowing she was as naked as
the day she was born and standing right behind him was enough to send his blood pressure sky-high.

The sound of her stepping into the spa
caused sweat to pop out on his forehead. He
hadn't anticipated remembering how he'd
sipped water droplets from her satiny skin
when they'd showered together. He gritted his
teeth and tried desperately to think of anything
but how her lithe wet body had felt against his.

"Oh, dear heavens that feels good," Karly
said, her tone appreciative. As if it was an afterthought, she added, "You can turn around
now."

Thankful that he had switched off the sub-
merged lights to keep her from seeing the obvious evidence of how she still affected him,

Blake sat down on the side of the lounge chair and took his time pulling off his boots and socks. Maybe if he gave himself a few minutes before he got into the water with her, he could get a grip on his suddenly nonexistent control.

When he stood up to unbuckle his belt and release the button at the waistband of his jeans, he thought he heard her moan softly. "Are you all right?" he asked, unzipping his fly to shove his jeans and boxer briefs down his legs.

He couldn't help but chuckle when Karly sent a little wave of water over the rock edge of the tub as she quickly whirled around to look away from where he was undressing. "I-I'm just…amazed at how wonderful this warm water feels."

"I think you'll have to agree, the hot tub was a good idea," he said, knowing that wasn't the real reason behind her moan.

But he kept that knowledge to himself. Pointing out that she was no more immune to him now than she had been in Las Vegas would only put her on the defensive and prevent him from learning why she had changed her mind about them.

By the time he had removed his clothes, he felt a little more in control of his body. So he walked over to the side of the heated spa and stepped into the bubbling water. Lowering himself to the stone seat beside her, he closed his eyes and took a deep breath as the soothing, heated water swirled around them. Just knowing that her nude body was only inches away from his was playing hell with his good intentions.

"This is an unusual hot tub," she commented. "I don't think I've ever seen one made out of stones. It looks so natural."

Nodding, he opened his eyes. "The owner told some pool designer what he wanted and the guy made it happen."

"Well, whoever the designer was, he did a wonderful job." She looked toward the curtain of water separating the hidden room from the pool. "This feels like we're in a tropical paradise."

"I'm pretty sure that was the plan," Blake said, smiling.

Her appreciation for his home and for the attention to detail that he'd put into it pleased him more than he would have thought. The fact that he had wanted to share it with her for the rest of their lives made her approval bittersweet.

Deciding it was a good time to get a few answers about why she'd changed her mind about them, he asked, "Have you always lived in Seattle?"

She turned her head to give him a puzzled look. "Where did that question come from?"

"Just wondering," he said, shrugging. He didn't want to give her the impression she was being interrogated. And asking her the questions he hadn't asked in Vegas would be a good way to keep his mind away from thoughts of her nude body.

"To satisfy your curiosity, I was born in New York City and with the exception of living in a small town in the Midwest for a few years, I was raised there," she said, answering his question. "From what you said about going to school in Eagle Fork, I assume you've always lived around here?"

He nodded. "Yup. And I take it the pony ride happened while you lived in the small town."

"Yes." She laughed. "I don't think I've ever heard of a market in Manhattan that has pony rides during their grand opening."

"Why did your family move from the city?" he asked, making sure to keep his tone from sounding too interested.

"My father was an industrial engineer and the company he worked for sent him to study and improve the productivity of one of their manufacturing plants." She stared at the waterfall. "He loved it in the Midwest, but my mother hated it."

"What about you?" he asked. "How did you feel about it?"

"To tell you the truth, I was really too young to have much of an opinion one way or the other," she commented. "And when my mother decided she'd had enough of small-town life, she took me back to New York and that was that."

"Your parents divorced?" he asked gently.

She nodded. "Unfortunately, I only saw my father a couple of times after we moved. He was killed in a car accident within a year after the divorce."

Without a second thought, Blake put his arm around her bare shoulders and pulled her to his side. "I'm sorry, Karly. I know how hard that is on a kid. I lost my mom when I was ten."

"I was only six when he died and all I really remember about him was that he worked a lot and he took me for ice cream more than my mother wanted him to," she said, her voice somber. He could tell it bothered her that she couldn't remember the man who helped to give her life.

"Dads have a tendency to do things moms

would rather they didn't," he said, chuckling. "I remember one time my mom gave my dad a hard time for taking my brother and me to Cheyenne Frontier Days and letting us eat so many corn dogs and so much cotton candy that we were sick for two days."

"My mother wasn't as afraid that I'd get sick as she was that I would gain weight," she explained. "Martina Ewing was an editor for one of the premier fashion magazines before we moved to the Midwest and she was determined that I would be in the industry, as well." She shook her head. "It never occurred to her that I might want to do something else with my life."

"Did your mother resume her career when you returned to New York?" he asked when she fell silent. He sensed there might be something about her parents splitting up that was relevant to their marriage situation. He just couldn't put his finger on what it was.

"She tried going back, but she'd been out of the loop long enough that she'd lost her place in the industry," Karly answered. "She blamed my dad for the loss of her career and never forgave him for it."

They both fell silent for a few minutes and Blake knew beyond a shadow of a doubt that her parents' marital problems had been a big influence on Karly. He wasn't sure exactly how it had factored into her decision to pursue a divorce, but he had every intention of finding out.

As he sat there pondering her reasoning, one thing became very apparent. He was sitting in a bubbling hot tub with her soft, nude body pressed closely to his. The lighted waterfall cast a dim glow into the tiny room, which only added to the intimacy of the moment. His reaction was not only predictable, but it was also inevitable.

With only a fleeting thought to the consequences, Blake pulled Karly closer and lowered his head. The feel of her water-slickened body rubbing against his was enough to send him into orbit, but the moment their mouths touched, a smoldering heat filled his lower belly and quickly sent liquid fire streaking through his veins. He briefly wondered how he could burn to a cinder while sitting in a tub of water.

When she sighed and brought her arms up to encircle his neck, it didn't even occur to him to resist deepening the kiss, and as he stroked her tongue with his, her sweet taste and eager response only heightened the need building inside of him. It was like nothing had changed since they were in Vegas. He was as hot for her now as he had been then. And he could tell she wanted him just as much.

Unfortunately, his timing was lousy. Making love to her right now could very well scare her into leaving the ranch without him getting to the bottom of what went wrong between them. Besides, he wasn't prepared to protect her. He hadn't come to the hot tub with seduction on his mind. And an unplanned pregnancy now would only add another wrinkle to an already complicated situation.

Easing away from the kiss, Blake held her close as he took several deep breaths. His hormones were racing through him like a herd of mustangs at a wild horse roundup and knowing there were no barriers between his body and hers wasn't making his decision to pull away any easier.

"It's probably time we got out of the hot tub and headed back to the foreman's cottage," he said halfheartedly.

"I—I think…you're right," she said, sounding just as reluctant as he felt.

Leaning back, he stared into her incredible blue eyes. "Karly, what…" He stopped and cleared his throat to keep from asking her what went wrong with them. Instead he declared,

"I'll get out and get dressed first. Then I'll wait for you out by the pool."

"That's a good idea," she agreed. "Thank you."

Damning his nobility, Blake got out of the hot tub before he could change his mind, quickly toweled himself dry and got dressed. Picking up his boots and socks, he made it a point not to look back at Karly, who was still sitting in the spa as he left the man-made cave. If he had looked back, he wasn't sure he would have been able to walk away.

As he sat down on the foot of one of the lounge chairs by the pool to pull on his socks and boots, Blake told himself he was doing the right thing—that making love to Karly again would only make things worse when he watched her drive away in a few days. But that reasoning didn't do a thing to lessen the need for her that still burned in his gut.

Rising to his feet, he took a deep breath. He might as well face facts. He wanted her—had never stopped wanting her. If he hadn't known that before, he sure as hell did now.

He rubbed the tension at the back of his neck. He could see a lot of cold showers in his near future and the first one would be tonight—as soon as they returned to the foreman's cottage.

* * *

"Blake, I think I'll leave to make the drive to Lincoln County after we have breakfast tomorrow morning," Karly said as he drove the truck away from the log mansion.

"I thought we had that settled," he said, staring straight ahead. "You were going to wait until the strike was done and fly to Spokane."

"I just think it would be for the best," she said, unwilling to admit out loud that she was in real danger of falling under his spell once again.

Sitting in the hot tub next to him, having him put his arm around her and feeling his naked body against hers had almost been her undoing. Even though she hadn't been able to see much in the dim light of the little cave housing the hot tub, her memory had filled in the blanks. In her mind, she had seen every well-defined muscle, every plane and valley of his impressive physique. Remembering how his strong arms had held her so securely and how gently he made love to her was overwhelming, and she shivered as a wave of desire coursed through every part of her.

"I know I shouldn't have kissed you." He took a deep breath and added, "Either in the barn or tonight in the hot tub. But it felt right and I'll be damned if I'm going to apologize for it."

She couldn't in good conscience allow him to shoulder all of the blame. "You wouldn't have kissed me if I hadn't let you."

His deep chuckle sent heat pulsing through her veins. "Yeah, I noticed you weren't protesting."

"That's the problem." She sighed. "I should have."

He glanced over at her. "Why didn't you?"

"I…wanted you to kiss me," she admitted.

"But you didn't want to want me kissing you." It wasn't a question.

"No."

"Sweetheart, a wife wanting her husband to kiss her is allowed," he said, reaching over to take her hand in his. The moment their palms touched a delightful tingling sensation streaked up her arm.

She did her best to ignore it and tried to focus on what he'd said. "That's the problem, Blake. Three months from now we'll be divorced. I shouldn't want you kissing me, not anymore."

He gave her hand a gentle squeeze. "Have you asked yourself why you do?"

His question took her by surprise. But as

she tried to think of an answer, she decided it probably wasn't wise to delve too deeply into the reason behind her wanting his affection. If she did, she was certain she wouldn't be all that comfortable with the answer.

"You're only going to be here a few more days, Karly," he said pragmatically. "And I give you my word that nothing is going to happen between us unless that's what you want. But I'm not going to lie to you and tell you it isn't what I want."

As he drove the truck up the lane to the foreman's cottage, Karly thought about what Blake had said. What *did* she want?

Eight months ago, she'd been confident she was making the right decision when she'd said yes to his marriage proposal. She had been certain at the time she married him that she loved Blake and wanted them to spend the rest of their lives together. But when she'd returned to Seattle her practical side had taken over. That's when she'd known ending things was the right call—for both of them.

She'd questioned falling in love with him so quickly and feared that their feelings for each other might not last. Then she'd thought about her parents. Her mother had been in love with her father, but in the end it hadn't been enough for her. She'd become bitter and resentful, and Karly had borne the brunt of that bitterness.

Karly loved her own career as an import buyer—loved the travel to foreign countries—and feared that love might not be enough for her, either, if she had to give up all of that. Had she been wrong about her feelings for her job? Could she have been happy being the wife of a ranch foreman in a remote part of Wyoming when all she'd ever known was living in a city with conveniences just steps from her apartment door?

She'd been so sure of everything when she left Seattle to come to the ranch for him to sign the new set of divorce papers. But then she'd seen him—stayed with him, had him treat her like his wife—and the doubts about her decision had set in.

She might have been able to keep things in perspective if she hadn't been stranded on the ranch by the airport workers' strike. She'd have gone back to Washington, filed the papers for the dissolution of their marriage and resumed her career with the confidence she was doing the right thing.

The trouble had come from seeing him again, being in his arms and experiencing the magic of his kiss. It all reminded her of what she'd wanted when she'd walked down that aisle in Vegas—what she was giving up—and had her questioning herself at every turn.

Had there been serious flaws in her reasoning? By insisting they continue with the divorce was she making the biggest mistake of her life? Would he even give her a second chance if she did want for them to try to make their marriage work?

Karly glanced over at Blake when he parked the truck beside the foreman's cottage. The way he held her—kissed her—he seemed open to rekindling what they'd found together in Las Vegas. But he hadn't once mentioned wanting her to change her mind. He'd even signed the divorce papers without a word of protest or even the slightest hesitation.

She sighed when he got out of the truck and she waited for him to walk around to open the passenger door. She wasn't nearly as sure of everything as she'd been when she arrived here. And the only way she was going to determine what was best would be to stay with Blake on the ranch and give herself the time to sort it all out.

Six

On Sunday morning when Blake walked back into the foreman's cottage after getting their breakfast from the bunkhouse cook, Karly was seated at the table waiting for him. "I thought you'd still be asleep," he said as he set the containers of food on the kitchen island.

"My phone woke me," she said, her tone pensive. He noticed her tightly clasped hands resting on the table in front of her. Her knuckles were white and she looked like she had something pretty heavy on her mind.

Without giving it a second thought, he walked over to where she sat, took her hands in his and pulled her to her feet. "What's wrong?" he asked, loosely holding her to him. He wasn't sure why, but it bothered him to think she might be worried about anything at all.

Instead of her backing away as he thought she might, she wrapped her arms around his waist and laid her head against his chest. "The strike at the Denver airport is over. The airline can get me on a flight out of Cheyenne tomorrow morning."

She didn't sound overly happy about it and he took that as a sign that despite what she'd said last night on the way home from the main house, she wanted to stay with him a little longer. And that was just fine with him. He told himself that he was okay with it because he hadn't yet discovered what had originally changed her mind about them. But if he was perfectly honest with himself, he would have to admit that he wanted to spend more time with her before he had to say goodbye and watch her drive out of his life for good. The way he saw it, having one more day with her was worth whatever hell he would have to face of a lifetime without her.

"You don't have to leave." He put his index finger beneath her chin to tilt her head up until their eyes met. "Why don't you stay a few more days?"

"I can't afford to miss work," she said, shaking her head. "I only have a couple of vacation days left and I'll need to use those for the stop in Lincoln County to file the...d-divorce."

She stumbled over the word and he would bet nearly every dime he had that she was starting to second-guess her decision. "Can you work from here?"

She looked thoughtful. "You mean telecommute?"

He nodded. "The signal here is good, but it's a lot better over at the main house. You could work from there."

"As nice as your boss is, I'm sure he'll draw the line at some stranger using up all of his bandwidth," she stated.

Blake shrugged. "Like I said, he's not staying there right now. When he had the Wi-Fi installed, he made sure it was unlimited usage with no slowdowns." He purposely omitted that Blake himself was one of the internet company's principal shareholders.

She looked thoughtful a moment before she shook her head. "I didn't bring my laptop."

"Not a problem," he said, smiling. He knew she was giving it serious consideration and he was determined to convince her to stay on the Wolf Creek Ranch a little longer. "You can use mine."

"Are you sure?" she asked. "You might have something on it that's private."

He shook his head. "I only use it for breeding records and to keep track of the cattle we'll be sending to market. There's more than enough room on the hard drive for anything you'll be doing and if you need a special program we can always download it."

"I'll have to call the office on Tuesday morning and explain that I'm going to be working from here for a few days," she said, her expression thoughtful. "I've telecommuted in the past, so it shouldn't be a problem to set it up. And I'll need to email one of my coworkers to have her send me a couple of files I'll need."

"Then it's settled," he said, refusing to acknowledge just how important it had become to him that she extended her stay. "After breakfast we'll go over to the mansion and get everything arranged in the office."

She frowned. "Blake, I know you say your boss is easygoing and won't mind, but I'm sure he'd have a big problem with me using his office."

"There's a writing desk in one of the upstairs bedrooms," he said, thinking quickly. "We'll just move over to the mansion and you can work out of that bedroom."

"That's even worse, Blake," she said, shaking her head. "We can't just move into your boss's home." She stared at him. "Who is this man and why do you insist on taking advantage of his good nature so often?"

He took a deep breath. He should tell her the truth. He'd boxed himself into a corner and he had nobody to blame but himself. If he told her now that he was the owner of the Wolf Creek Ranch she thought he was taking advantage of, she'd think he had been playing her for a fool or, worse yet, that he had been trying to hide his assets from her because of the divorce. But the longer he waited, the worse it was going to be when she did find out.

Deciding he needed to dial things back a little while he tried to figure out the best time and way to tell Karly he was the man in question, Blake backtracked. "You're right. We don't want to take advantage while he's away from the mansion. But there's one place that I know he won't mind you using."

"Where's that?" she asked, seemingly distracted from finding out who the owner was—at least for the time being.

"There's a table in the library just off the family room that would be the perfect place for you to work," he said, bringing his hand up to twine his fingers in her silky blond hair. "It's quiet in there and you won't have to worry about anyone interrupting you or you using a room the boss would find objectionable." He lowered his head to brush her perfect lips with his. "And when you take a break for lunch all you'll have to do is walk down the hall to the kitchen and Silas will make you something to eat."

Unable to resist, he gave in to temptation and settled his mouth over hers. He knew he was playing with fire and would most likely get burned by his weakness for her. But he couldn't seem to control himself when he was around Karly. It had been that way in Vegas and it was that way now. Whenever he was with her, all he could think about was holding her close, kissing her until she sagged against him and making love to her until they both collapsed from the sheer pleasure of being together.

As he deepened the kiss, she put her arms around his neck and melted against him. Her soft curves pressed against his rapidly hardening body and the sweetness that was uniquely Karly caused his heart to thump against his chest like a jungle drum. No other woman had ever fit against him so perfectly or responded to his kiss as readily.

When she moaned softly and snuggled even closer, he realized that she felt his arousal straining against his fly. The fact that she was as hot for him as he was for her sent adrenaline pumping through his veins at the speed of light. Whatever caused her to want out of their brief marriage apparently had nothing to do with her desire for him. That was as strong, if not stronger, than it had been when they'd taken that trip down the aisle at that little chapel on the Vegas strip.

Barely able to resist the urge to take off both of their clothes and make love to her right there in the kitchen, he forced himself to ease away from the kiss. "Sweetheart, as much as I'd like to take this all the way to a satisfying conclusion for both of us, I think we'd better take a time-out."

Her smooth porcelain cheeks wore the blush of passion and he sensed that if he hadn't called a halt to things, she probably wouldn't have, either. That's when he knew beyond a shadow of doubt that there was every likelihood they would be making love before she left. And soon.

"I, uh, y-yes." She looked a little dazed. "I'll get flatware and coffee mugs."

While she walked over to get the items from the cabinets, Blake took a deep breath and set the two plates of bacon, scrambled eggs and hash browns on the table, along with a thermos of coffee. How the hell could a man feel like he'd done the right thing and, at the same time, regret doing it?

He wasn't sure. But he knew now that he needed to come clean with Karly and tell her that he owned the ranch before things progressed any further between them. Karly was intelligent and she'd already started questioning why he kept taking advantage of the mysteriously absent ranch owner. It was just a matter of time before she figured it out or someone unwittingly told her.

And the worst part of all, his reasons for keeping it from her were making less sense, even to him, with each passing day.

Karly sat at the library table in the log mansion and looked around at the volumes of books on the shelves lining the room. The owner's tastes were eclectic and included ranching manuals, nonfiction, autobiographies and novels by some of the most popular, bestselling authors of the past one hundred years.

As she continued to look around, she couldn't help but smile. Unlike a lot of home libraries, which felt gloomy and heavy with the knowledge of the ages, the room felt cozy and extremely inviting. So much so that she could imagine herself spending endless hours on a rainy or snowy day curled up with a good book and a warm, comfy afghan on the big leather sofa in front of a crackling fire in the stone fireplace.

She rose to her feet and walked over to look out one of the windows at the surrounding mountains. Now that she'd visited the ranch, she could understand why Blake had told her he couldn't leave Wyoming for life in a bustling city. The land was beautiful and although she loved the green beauty of both the Cascade and Olympic Mountains, she couldn't look out any of the windows in her apartment and see them. If she wanted to enjoy the lush scenery, she had to take a ferry across Puget Sound or drive out of the city to the thick forests beyond.

But here on the Wolf Creek Ranch, every window had a spectacular view of the Laramie Mountains and experiencing nature took little more than walking out the door.

She sighed. When she had returned to Seattle after their whirlwind courtship and wedding, she had reasoned that living so far from a city would eventually end her and Blake's marriage the way it had with her parents'. She'd even convinced herself that she was doing what was best for both of them—that there would be less emotional pain by ending it so early in the union than there would be a few years down the line.

But she had to admit that although most of her conclusions made sense, they weren't her only motivation for insisting on a divorce. The main, most compelling reason that she'd refused to move to Wyoming with her new husband had been due to fear—not that he would fail her, but that she would fail him.

She had been afraid she would eventually feel about Blake the way her mother had felt about her father. And that was something she wasn't going to let happen. She cared too much for him to blame him for things he had no control over.

Martina Ewing had become a bitter, resentful woman once she returned to New York and learned she had lost her place in the world of high fashion. Until her death just a few years ago, Karly's mother had blamed Karly's father for the loss of her career, her unhappiness and just about everything else unpleasant that happened in her life. She still managed to find fault with him, even though he'd passed away not long after they divorced. Karly sometimes wondered if her mother had even blamed him for leaving her saddled with a child to raise.

But in Karly's attempt to protect Blake from the possibility that she would turn out to be as unreasonable as her mother, had she allowed her fear to deprive them of a real chance at happiness?

"It's beautiful, isn't it?" Blake asked, wrapping his arms around her waist and pulling her back against his solid chest.

Startled, she jumped. "I didn't know you had returned to the house."

After they'd finished breakfast, he had given her his laptop and driven them over to the mansion to set up her workspace in the library. Once he'd made sure the internet connection was the speed she needed, he'd told her he was going out to see that the indoor arena's floor had been properly prepared for the training of a new stallion and left her to familiarize herself with his computer and to download a couple of programs she would need to do her job. But she suspected that had been an excuse to give her the time and space to think about the direction her visit had taken and what she wanted to do about it.

They were both aware that the chemistry between them was as strong as ever and that it wouldn't take much to send it spiraling out of control. It had almost happened last night in the hot tub and then again this morning when he kissed her.

"Did you get everything ready to start to work?" he asked, sending a wave of goose bumps shimmering over her arms.

She nodded. "And I went ahead and sent the email to my coworker so it's waiting for her when she arrives at the office Tuesday morning."

"I'm glad you'll be here at the mansion." He brushed her long hair out of the way to nibble kisses down the column of her neck. "I have to start working in the arena with the new stallion and I'd hate for you to spend the day alone over at the foreman's cottage."

"I was going to ask you about that," she said, attempting to get her mind off how good he was making her feel. "Why are the barns and corrals at the foreman's cottage instead of here at the main ranch house?"

His low chuckle caused her knees to wobble.

"Sweetheart, in the warmer months, having the barns and livestock a quarter of a mile away makes entertaining guests out on the patio a lot more pleasant."

"Oh, I hadn't thought about the dust and the noise the animals make," she commented.

"Along with Essence of Barnyard floating on the breeze. It doesn't inspire people to attend a cookout or pool party," he said, laughing.

Smiling, she nodded. "It makes perfect sense now." She frowned suddenly and turned in his arms to face him. "But the barn is no more than fifty yards from the cottage and I haven't noticed a lot of dust or barnyard odors at the foreman's cottage."

"When the owner's family established the Wolf Creek Ranch back in the late 1800s, they made sure to build the barns and outbuildings downwind of the house." He shrugged. "I think that held true for most ranches back then. They figured out which way the wind usually blows and planned their layout accordingly."

"So the foreman's cottage was the original ranch house?" she asked. She hadn't really thought about it before, but he had mentioned the owner building the mansion after he bought the ranch a couple of years ago.

He nodded. "I think every generation has remodeled and built onto it, but the original homestead is in the foreman's cottage somewhere."

"How do you know so much about the ranch?" she asked, puzzled by his knowledge of its history.

He looked a little taken aback by her question. "My family has lived here...as long as the owners have." Although not overly common anymore, she'd heard that in years past it wasn't all that unusual for generations of cowboys to work for the same ranch.

"By the way, I don't recall hearing you mention the name of the man who owns the ranch," she said, frowning.

She hadn't much more than gotten the words out than Blake lowered his head and pulled her to him. With his mouth moving so masterfully over hers, it suddenly didn't matter who owned the ranch. All she cared about was having him continue to hold her to his broad chest, kiss her until she was breathless and so much more.

That thought should have had her pushing away from his secure embrace. Wanting to make love and wanting their marriage to work out were two entirely different things. Or were they?

But when Blake deepened the kiss, Karly abandoned all thought in favor of losing herself in the way he was making her feel. A delicious warmth flowed throughout her body the moment his tongue touched hers and as he explored her with such tender care, her knees failed her completely. He caught her to him and the feel of his rock-hard body sent waves of longing all the way to her core.

Lost in the overwhelming need he was creating, her heart skipped a beat when he brought his hand up along her side to gently cup her breast. The feel of his thumb teasing her through the layers of her T-shirt and bra only intensified her desire, making her restless and impatient to feel his calloused hands touching her bare skin.

When he broke the kiss to nibble his way along her jaw, then down her neck to the hollow below her ear, Karly couldn't stop herself from vocalizing what she wanted. "Blake, please."

"What do you want, Karly?" he asked as he continued to tease her.

"You. I…want you."

"And I want you, sweetheart," he said, leaning back to look at her. His brown gaze held hers as a slow smile curved his lips. "Let's go back to the foreman's cottage."

Needing him more than she needed her next breath, Karly let him lead her through the mansion and out the front door to his truck. On the ride back to the foreman's cottage, reality began to intrude and by the time Blake parked the truck at the side of the house, she had begun to question her sanity. She longed for him to make love to her—and, to her own surprise, she longed for him to *love* her again— but she needed him to understand the depth of the fears and insecurities that had held her back for the past eight months. Before they could move forward into a future together, she had to explain about her past.

When he got out and walked around to help her down from the passenger side of the truck, she had to let him know about her apprehension. She had to try to make him understand so he could forgive her for not believing in them. "Blake, we need to talk before we do anything impulsive."

He stared at her for several long moments and the heated look in his dark brown eyes stole her breath. "Karly, do you want me?"

"Y-yes. B-but—"

"I give you my word that we'll talk later," he said, putting his arm around her waist and tucking her to his side as he walked them into the house. "But not now. I haven't made love to my wife in over eight months and I've needed you every second of every day since we left Vegas."

His words sent a fresh wave of longing from the top of her head to the soles of her feet. She hadn't realized it before she came to Wyoming, before she'd spent this time on the land he loved so much, but she felt the same way.

She needed him with every fiber of her being. She didn't know how she'd gone these long eight months without him. And after they made love they could discuss why she had refused to join him here, why she'd insisted a divorce was the right decision. They could figure out where they were headed in the future after they made love. Right now, she craved the magic of his touch and the overwhelming pleasure of being one with him.

She could hardly believe what she was about to say. But as she stared up at him, she knew that from the moment she'd decided to bring him the divorce papers in person, she'd never really had a choice.

"Blake, please take me upstairs and make me forget how long it's been."

Seven

When Blake opened the door to the room she'd been using since her arrival at the ranch, memories of the first time they'd made love caused Karly's stomach to flutter with anticipation. It had been so long since he'd touched her and for the past eight months she'd lain in bed every night missing the feel of his skin pressed to hers, their bodies entwined in an embrace as old as time. A shiver slid up her spine and her heart skipped a beat at the thought.

When he closed the door behind them, he reached for her. Neither of them said a word as they stood with their arms around each other and simply enjoyed the moment.

As he drew back to look at her, he placed her hands on his shoulders for support before he removed her boots and socks, then pulled off his.

"Karly, I want you to know there hasn't been anyone since we left Vegas," he said, his brown eyes reflecting the truth in his words as he straightened to his full height and took her back into his arms. He brought his hand up to gently caress her cheek. "When we got married, I vowed that I would be faithful to you. And as far as I'm concerned, I'm still your husband until I receive papers telling me otherwise."

She nodded. "That's the way I felt about it, as well."

Leaning forward, he brushed her lips with his. "I promised you we would talk about all that later, and I meant it. But right now, I intend to get reacquainted with my wife's beautiful body." Her pulse sped up when he reached for the hem of her T-shirt and slowly pulled it up and over her head.

"I can't let you be the only one having all the fun," she said, tugging his chambray shirt from the waistband of his jeans. She unfastened the top snap and slowly, methodically released the closures. She placed her hands beneath each side of his open shirt to brush it from his shoulders and her breath caught. She'd always found the hard ridges and valleys of his well-developed chest and abdomen fascinating. "Your body is perfect."

"If you want to talk about perfection—" he paused and reached behind her, releasing the clasp of her bra "—you're the one who's stunning."

The appreciation in his dark eyes stole her breath. But when he cupped her breasts with both hands, then kissed each hardened tip, her knees wobbled and she had to place her palms on his chest to steady herself.

The moment her fingers came into contact with the thick pads of his pectoral muscles, he shuddered and she knew he loved having her touch him as much as she loved having him touch her. Inspired to give him as much pleasure as he was giving her, she continued her exploration of his body and let her hands drift down to his belt buckle.

When she paused to glance up at him, he grinned. "Don't stop now, sweetheart. This is just starting to get interesting."

"That's one of the things that I've always

found amazing about you," she said, unbuck-
ling the tooled leather strap of his belt.

"What's that?" he asked, his breathing
sounding a bit labored.

"You openly encourage me to do the same
things to you that you're doing to me," she said,
releasing the button at the top of his jeans.

"That's a big part of making love, sweetheart" he said, teasing her nipples with the
pads of his thumbs. "It's about trust and the
freedom to learn what we like and how to bring
the most pleasure to each other."

She wasn't all that experienced, but she had
a feeling not all men were willing to be vulnerable with their partner. Her heart swelled with
emotion at the thought that Blake was secure
enough in his manhood to trust her that much
when they made love.

When she smiled and took hold of the tab
at the top of his fly, he drew in a deep breath.
"Don't get me wrong. I love what you intend to
do," he said, his smile so sexy it sent her pulse
racing. "But an excited man and a metal zipper can be a real bad combination."

She gazed up at him as she cased one hand
inside his jeans between his cotton underwear and the zipper. "Maybe this will keep
you safe," she said, delighting in the heat she

detected in his eyes as she eased the offending zipper down over his insistent erection.

But she hadn't anticipated the effect his arousal would have on her. The feel of the hard ridge against the backs of her fingers caused heat to flow through her veins and her insides to feel as if they had turned to warm pudding.

By the time she finished the task of un-zipping him, she felt as if she might go up in a puff of smoke. But when she looked up at Blake's handsome face, his eyes were closed and a muscle worked along his lean jaw as if he might be in pain.

"Are you all right?" she asked, concerned.

He opened his eyes and his slow, sexy grin sent a shiver up her spine. "Sweetheart, do you have any idea what it does to a man when a woman touches him like that?"

"Even through your underwear?" she asked playfully.

Laughing, he nodded. "It's a thin barrier and a real sensitive area. I'd have to be a eunuch not to react."

Moving her hands to his sides, she carefully pushed his jeans and boxer briefs down his lean hips and muscular thighs. When she lowered them to his ankles, she caressed the backs of his knees and strong calves. Rewarded with his deep groan, she realized that something as simple as skimming her hands down the backs of his legs could bring him pleasure.

When he stepped out of the denim and cotton, then kicked his clothing to the side, she bit her lower lip to keep a tiny moan from escaping. "You're absolutely beautiful. I've always thought so."

Shaking his head, he pulled her to him. "Women are all gentle curves and soft, smooth skin. That's beautiful. But men are too angular, hard and hairy to be anything but passable at best."

"Don't sell yourself short," she said, gazing up at him.

He surprised her when he raised one dark eyebrow. "Really? I'm standing here without a stitch of clothes on and you had to mention the word *short*?"

In truth, he was a man who had nothing whatsoever to be insecure about and the humor in his eyes told her he knew it. She couldn't help but giggle as she placed her hands on his wide chest.

"I suppose that was a poor choice of words. But do you really want to talk about my word choices now?" she asked, running her index finger down the shallow valley between his chest and navel.

"No." He kissed his way from her cheek down her neck to her collarbone. "I fully intend to take the rest of your clothes off, lay you on that bed over there and spend the rest of today and tonight loving every inch of you."

When he lifted his head, his gaze caught and held hers as he reached to release the button at her waist, then lowered the zipper. His smile held so much promise as he ran his index finger along the elastic waistband of her bikini panties, Karly thought she might melt right then and there.

As he began to ease her jeans and underwear over her hips and down her legs, the tantalizing abrasion of his calloused hands on her skin caused her heart to skip several beats and a delicious shiver to run through her. When she stepped out of the garments, the heated appreciation in his dark eyes took her breath away.

"Gorgeous," he said, stepping forward to wrap his arms around her.

The feel of her breasts pressed to his hard, hair-roughened chest caused her knees to give way. But when he caught her and pulled her more fully against him, his strong arousal nestled against her soft lower belly. The feel of it made Karly's head spin.

Without a word he led her over to the bed and pulled back the comforter. "I'll be right back," he said, walking over to where their discarded clothing lay on the floor.

As she watched, he picked up his jeans to get something from his wallet. When he returned, he placed a foil packet on the bedside table and stretched out on the mattress beside her.

Gathering her into his arms, he smiled. "I'm assuming you still aren't on any kind of birth control."

"There hasn't been a reason for it," she said honestly. She'd intended to talk with her doctor about it once she returned from Las Vegas, but when it seemed that their marriage had ended she hadn't bothered.

"It's not a problem," he said, kissing her forehead. "It's my job to take care of you and protect you, even if that protection is from me."

"Thank you," she said, touching his lean cheek. She'd been so caught up in the moment, she hadn't given protection a second thought.

He stared at her and the look in his eyes was breathtaking before a slow smile curved his lips. He lowered his head to kiss her with a tenderness that brought tears to her eyes. No

other man had ever shown her so much rever-
ence or been as devoted to bringing her pleasure as Blake. And in that moment, she knew
that no other man ever would.

When he deepened the kiss, he brought his
hand up to cup her breast and tease her nipple
with gentle care. Her pulse sped up as ribbons
of desire coursed through every part of her and
an ache began to form deep inside. A mixture
of impatience and anticipation filled her as he
moved his hand to caress his way down her
side to her hip then her knee.

As he continued to stroke her tongue with
his, he slowly moved his calloused palm along
the inside of her thigh. When he touched her, it
felt as if an electric current skipped over every
nerve in her body and she couldn't stop a tiny
moan from escaping.

Needing to touch him as he was touching
her, she moved her hands from his wide chest
down his abdomen to his lean flanks. She felt
him shudder against her and, encouraged by
his reaction, she moved her hands lower. When
she found him, she stroked his length and
tested the heaviness below. He suddenly went
perfectly still a moment before a deep groan
rumbled up from his chest. He broke away
from the kiss to take several deep breaths.

"Sweetheart, as much as I hate to say it, I think you'd better stop…and let me catch my breath," he said haltingly. He trapped her hands in his and placed them back on his chest. "If you don't, you're going to be disappointed and I'm going to be real embarrassed."

"It's been so long," she said, knowing that if they didn't make love soon she was going to go out of her mind with longing. "I need you, Blake."

"And I need you, Karly," he said, reaching for the foil packet he'd placed on the bedside table earlier. Arranging their protection, he nudged her knees apart and rose over her. "I promise next time it won't be as rushed."

If she could have found her voice she would have told him that she couldn't have waited any longer. But words were impossible when he guided himself to her and she felt him slowly begin to fill her.

As her body stretched to accommodate his, her chest tightened with emotion. She had never felt as complete as she did when Blake made them one. It had been that way in Las Vegas—it was that way now. And she knew in her heart that's the way it would always be. He was her man—her other half—and no amount of time or distance or fear or insecurity would ever change that.

Her heart stalled as she realized she'd fallen in love with him all over again. But as she stared up at his handsome face, she knew that wasn't true. If she was honest with herself, she'd have to admit she'd never fallen out of love with him.

"You feel so damned good," Blake said, oblivious to her realization.

Deciding to think about her sudden insight later, Karly noticed his clenched jaw and the strained expression on his handsome face. It reflected his struggle for control and his determination to bring her pleasure before he found his own.

"Please make love to me, Blake," she said, wrapping her arms around him as she arched her body into his.

Groaning, he lowered his lips to hers and to her delight, he began to rock against her. Slow and gentle, she was certain his movements were calculated to bring her the most pleasure he possibly could. He made her feel as if she was the most cherished woman on earth and that it was his privilege to be with her.

But all too soon the tension he was building within her gathered into a coil of longing in her most feminine parts. Blake must have sensed her readiness because he increased the depth and strength of his strokes. Just when she thought her body would shatter from the exquisite tightening inside of her, she was suddenly set free. Pleasure flowed through every cell in her body and she felt as if she might faint from the beautiful sensations that seemed to go on forever.

As she slowly began to drift back to reality, Karly felt Blake's body surge into her one final time. He tightened his arms around her as if she was his lifeline and held her to him as he found his own shuddering release.

When he buried his head in the pillow beside her, she stroked the dark brown hair at the nape of his neck and reveled in their differences. His weight felt absolutely wonderful pressed against her and she felt surrounded by his much bigger body.

"I'm too heavy for you, sweetheart," he said, levering himself up on his forearms. He brushed a strand of hair from her cheek as he smiled down at her. "Are you all right?"

"I'm wonderful," she said, nodding.

"You can add *amazing* to that, as well as *exciting* and *beautiful*," he stated, brushing her lips with his. When he moved to her side, he pulled her to him and covered them both with the comforter. "It's been so long since I made love to you, I'm afraid my control wasn't what it should have been. I give you my word that the next time I'll make sure to give you more pleasure."

She shivered with anticipation at the thought of having him make love to her again. "As much as I love that idea, I think it would be best if we discussed a few things first," she said, knowing that even though this had been wonderful, everything had become a lot more complicated.

When he failed to respond, she moved her head from where it was pillowed on his shoulder to look up at him. His eyes were closed and she could tell by the movement of his broad chest that he had fallen asleep.

Karly kissed his chin and closed her eyes. He was probably exhausted from working with the stallion he had been training most of the day.

She yawned and snuggled closer to him. It might be for the best that he'd fallen asleep before they could talk. She needed to come to terms with the newfound knowledge that she was still in love with her husband, as well as decide what she wanted to do about that insight.

Did she have the courage to ask him to put the divorce on hold for a while to see if they could make their marriage work? Was that what she really wanted? Could he forgive her for the mistake she'd made in thinking their marriage would lead to her resenting him as her mother had resented her father? What would she do if she asked him for another chance and he decided that wasn't what he wanted?

She yawned again and felt the shadows of sleep begin to tug at her. Maybe if she rested for a while, she'd be able to think more clearly and the answers would come to her. They had to. Happiness for the rest of her life might very well depend on it.

The following evening, Blake took a swig of his beer as he watched his wife chatting and laughing with Tori Laughlin across the patio at the Rusty Spur Ranch house. Karly seemed to be having a good time, and he couldn't help but wonder if she would be around for the next get-together with his friends and their guests.

They hadn't talked about the future beyond agreeing that she would stay a few more days and she hadn't seemed any more ready to discuss what would happen after that than he was. Before they made love, he had promised her they would talk afterward. But they'd both fallen asleep and when they woke up together in bed, nature had taken its course once again. They'd spent the rest of the night reacquainting themselves with each other's bodies and that morning they had awakened just in time to get ready to leave for the late-afternoon barbecue.

"You've really got it bad for her, don't you?" Eli Laughlin asked, walking up to stand next to Blake.

"Yeah, I guess I do," he admitted.

"She seems real nice," Eli commented. "When did the two of you meet?"

"During the Nationals Finals in Vegas before Christmas," he said, never taking his eyes off Karly. He took another swig of his beer. "That's when we got married."

When he'd called Eli a few days before to tell his friend he would be bringing a guest to the get-together, Blake had explained that she wasn't aware he owned the Wolf Creek Ranch and that he'd like to keep it that way. As he expected, Eli had immediately agreed. But Blake had known that at some point he'd need to explain his strange request and tell Eli that he and Karly were married.

In the middle of taking a drink of his beer, Eli choked and Blake reached over to pound him on the back. When his friend stopped coughing, he stared at Blake like he'd sprouted another head.

"You got married," Eli repeated as if he couldn't quite believe what Blake had just said.

Blake nodded and explained the events leading up to the current situation he and Karly found themselves in. "But filing for the divorce is on hold—at least until the end of the week."

Eli nodded. "That gives you a little time to figure out how you're going to ask her to stay—and how to tell her you own the Wolf Creek. You're also going to have to tell her why you kept that from her in the first place."

Watching his wife play with the Laughlin's two-year-old son, Aaron, Blake tried to imagine having a family with Karly. If her interaction with the toddler was any indication, she loved kids and would be everything he could possibly want for the mother of his children.

"Any suggestions about how I should go about handling all of that?" he asked, grinning.

Blake had known his friend would be the last to pass judgment on the way Blake and

Karly met and married. Eli and Tori hadn't gotten together in the usual way, either. And Blake had been confident that Eli wouldn't question his reasoning for keeping his wealth out of the equation. Before he met Tori, Eli had dealt with his own share of unscrupulous women going after his bank account.

Eli laughed. "You know better than to ask me for advice when it comes to women. I'm sure you remember what a stubborn jackass I was when Tori and I got married. I just thank the good Lord above that she loved me enough to give me a second chance."

"And look at you now," Blake agreed, laughing with his friend. "You're still a jackass, just a little less stubborn than you used to be."

"It takes one to know one," Eli retorted.

"What are you two laughing about this time?" Tori asked.

Looking up, Blake grinned as he watched the women and the toddler walking toward them. "I was just agreeing with your husband that he's a jackass."

"I was telling him that it takes a jackass to know one," Eli explained.

Tori laughed. "Well, it's nice to know some things never change. But right now, I need to steal Eli for a few minutes. The band has arrived and he needs to let them know where to set up while I take Aaron inside for a few minutes to change him into his pajamas."

"She said he'd be asleep before the band finished their first song," Karly commented as Tori carried the little boy inside the house.

Putting his arm around her shoulders, Blake pulled Karly to his side. "Are you having a good time?"

When she smiled up at him, it caused a hitch in his breathing. He suddenly wished they were back at the foreman's cottage, where he could spend the rest of the evening making love to her.

"I'm having a wonderful time," she said, sounding happy and relaxed. "I really like your friends. I'm just sorry I didn't get to meet your brother. Tori said he was supposed to be here, but was called away on business."

"Sean used to be a special agent with the FBI," Blake said, nodding. "They still get in touch with him sometimes to act as an independent consultant on certain types of cases."

"That sounds fascinating," she said, sounding genuinely interested. "Is your brother still involved in law enforcement?"

"Yes and no," he answered, setting his empty beer bottle on one of the patio tables to take her in his arms. "He's a private investigator now. But when he was with the Bureau he was a crisis negotiator. He gets calls from law enforcement agencies all over Wyoming and the surrounding states when they have a situation that requires his expertise." He leaned close to nibble kisses along the side of her neck. "But I don't want to talk about Sean right now. I want to discuss when you think it would be acceptable for us to leave for home."

She shivered against him and he knew she was anticipating the night ahead of them the same as he was. "I think we could leave after a couple of dances, since we have an hour-and-a-half drive to get back to the ranch."

"I'll be right back," he said suddenly as he released her and started across the patio to where the band was getting ready to start playing. When he reached the frontman, Blake pulled his wallet from the hip pocket of his jeans and took out a couple of hundred dollars. He handed the money to the man. "I'd really appreciate it if you could make the first couple of songs slow ones."

"Hey, for two hundred dollars we'll make the whole first set slow ones," the man answered as he pocketed the money.

"After the first two, you can play whatever

you want," Blake said, grinning. "Just make sure what you play is slow and good to dance to."

The man nodded. "You got it."

Blake walked back to where Karly stood and draped his arm across her shoulders. "Two slow dances and we're out of here."

"You didn't," she said, her voice filled with laughter.

"Yup, I sure did." He brushed his lips over hers. "I wasn't leaving anything to chance."

When she rose up on tiptoes, she whispered, "Don't tell anyone, but I'm not the least bit sorry."

Ten minutes later, when the band broke into a popular slow country love song, Blake led Karly out to the section of the patio that had been designated as the dance floor. Taking her into his arms, he swayed her back and forth in time with the music. The feel of her body aligned with his and the sensual brushing of her lower stomach against his steadily growing arousal had him wishing it had been one and done, instead of the two dances they'd decided were socially acceptable.

His heart stalled when she put her arms around his neck and pressed herself closer. "You're making me a little crazy, sweetheart," he warned.

"Only a little?" Her sexy smile sent his blood pressure sky-high. "I guess I'll just have to try a bit harder to make you a lot crazy."

Blake swallowed around the cotton clogging his throat in order to get his vocal cords to work as he looked around to find the Laughlins. When he spotted them talking to some of their guests, he took her by the hand and started toward the couple.

"Where are we going?" Karly asked, sounding like she already knew.

"To thank Eli and Tori for having us over." Giving her a quick kiss, Blake grinned. "Social conventions be damned, sweetheart. We're heading back home where we can both be as crazy as we want to be."

Eight

The moment he closed the door to the master bedroom in the foreman's cottage, Blake took Karly into his arms and captured her mouth with his. The hour-and-a-half drive from the Rusty Spur Ranch had taken its toll and he was wound up tighter than a two-dollar watch. Every nerve in his body was on high alert and he ached with the need to once again claim her as his wife.

His wife. Even the words felt right and if he'd had any doubts about marrying her before, they had been erased this evening. Watching her with his friends—seeing her play with little Aaron—had been enough to convince him that Karly was the woman for him. She fit in perfectly and he could tell that she and Tori would end up becoming best friends.

If this was even a glimpse of what their lives would be like as husband and wife, he'd be the happiest man alive for the rest of his days. And he fully intended to make sure she was the happiest woman.

Deepening the kiss, he gently stroked her tongue and explored her soft, sweet recesses. Her taste and eager response to the caress were all he could have hoped for. Reaching down, he tugged the tail of her T-shirt from the waistband of her jeans.

Her warm, satiny skin was like a fine piece of silk beneath his calloused palms. Easing away from the kiss, he skimmed his lips along her jawline and down her neck to the fluttering pulse at the base of her throat. "Sweetheart, I'd like to go slow and love every inch of you. But I need you so much right now, I'm not sure that's going to be possible."

She caught his face with her delicate hands and lifted his head until their gazes met. "You can go slow the next time, Blake. I need you now."

"Thank God," he said, burying his face in

her silky blond hair. "I don't think I could wait much longer, even if my life depended on it."

"I feel the same way. I thought I would burst into flames when we were on the dance floor and I felt how much you needed me." She shivered and he knew it had nothing to do with being chilled. "But I want you to do something for me."

Without a second thought, he nodded. "Anything for you, Karly."

"Let *me* make love to *you*," she said, giving him a look that sent his hormones racing through his veins at the speed of light. "Do you mind?"

What man in his right mind would turn down a beautiful woman doing incredibly sexy things to his body?

"I need you to promise me something, Karly," he said, pulling her close for a quick kiss.

"Wh-what's that?" she asked, sounding a little short of breath.

"If I tell you to stop whatever you're doing, can you give me your word that you will?"

She looked confused. "All right. But I don't understand—"

"I want us to finish this race together," he said, grinning.

He could tell she understood his meaning when she smiled. "I want that, too. I promise."

"Good." Stepping back, he held his arms wide. "I'm all yours, sweetheart."

Karly wasted no time in pointing to the side of the bed. "If you'll sit down, I'll take your boots off."

Looking forward to seeing what she had in mind, he did as she requested. He swallowed hard when she turned her back to him, straddled one of his legs and bent over. But when she started tugging on his boot and her delightful little bottom bobbed mere inches in front of his face, Blake was pretty sure he was going to have a coronary. By the time his boots and socks lay on the floor beside the bed, sweat had popped out on his forehead and his upper lip, and he felt like he just might need CPR.

"Sweetheart, why don't we take off our clothes and get into bed," he said, forcing himself to breathe as he stood up to unbuckle his belt. "Otherwise, I'm not going to last long enough to get to the main event."

"I think that would be a good idea," she said, sounding a little winded herself.

"I give you my word that I'll let you take my clothes off me another time when I'm not so revved up," he said, making quick work of his clothing.

He made it a point to keep his gaze averted while she removed hers. If he hadn't, he wasn't sure he wouldn't have gone up in a blaze of glory.

As Karly got into bed, he reached into his jeans for one of the condoms he'd remembered to get from his medicine cabinet when they were over at the mansion the day before. Placing it on the bedside table, he stretched out beside her.

When he started to pull her to him, she shook her head. "Remember, this is all about me giving you pleasure," she said, her smile causing another wave of heat to course from the top of his head to the soles of his feet.

"Just keep in mind that I'm only human and I do…have my limits," he said, feeling like he had been branded when she placed her hand on his chest.

When he cupped one of her perfect breasts, she closed her eyes and nodded. "I've almost reached mine, as well."

Just knowing that she was as turned on as he was had him clenching his teeth in an effort to slow down his overly active libido. But when she reached over to take the packet from the bedside table and carefully opened it, Blake closed his eyes and held his breath. He'd never had a woman do what Karly was planning to do and he could only hope that he had enough strength to hold on to what little control he had left.

At the first touch of her fingers to the most sensitive part of his body, Blake felt like he'd been treated to the business end of a cattle prod. He groaned and tried to think of something—anything—to take his mind off what the woman of his dreams was doing for him.

"Are you all right?" she asked when he let loose with a deep groan.

He nodded as he reached to take her hands in his. "I think you'd better give me...a minute."

"You need to catch your breath?" she asked.

"Yeah, we can...call it that," he said, breathing deeply in an effort to release some of the tension gripping him. When he felt like he had regained a degree of control, he warned, "I'm not going to be able to take much more, sweetheart."

"I can't, either," she said, rising to her knees.

His heart stopped completely when she straddled his hips and guided him into her. As he watched, she lowered herself onto him and just the sight of her body taking him in was mind-blowing. But the feel of her warmth surrounding him caused his body to respond with a tightening that left him feeling light-headed.

He watched her close her eyes as if she savored being one with him. Humbled that a woman as loving and beautiful as Karly would even want to be with him, he knew beyond a shadow of doubt that he still loved her.

It made him more determined than ever to find out what happened after she returned to Seattle. Whatever it was they'd find a way to work through it. And he could only hope she'd be able to forgive him for not telling her about himself sooner and give him a chance to make it up to her.

But he didn't have time to dwell on what he was going to do about his self-discovery and whatever obstacles they still faced. As he watched the woman who owned his heart, she opened her eyes, gave him a smile that caused his chest to tighten with emotion and slowly began to move against him.

He placed his hands on her hips and held on as the friction of their bodies increased the pressure building inside of him. He could tell

Karly was experiencing the same sensations from the blush of passion on her porcelain cheeks and the rapt light in her big blue eyes.

As he felt himself reaching the point where his satisfaction was inevitable, Karly's tiny feminine muscles tightened around him a moment before her head fell back and she gasped from the intense sensations flowing through her. That's when Blake took control of the pace and did his best to give her as much pleasure as he possibly could before his own release set him free. Groaning, he shuddered as he gave up his essence to the woman he loved.

When Karly collapsed on his chest, he wrapped his arms around her and held her to him as their bodies cooled and their breathing returned to normal. "Are you doing okay?" he whispered close to her ear.

"That was incredible," she said, raising her head to kiss his chin.

"You're incredible." He enjoyed the feel of her lying on top of him and the connection they still shared. "Next time I promise you can take my clothes off and have your wicked way with me," he said, chuckling. "But I was so turned on, I wouldn't have lasted five minutes if you'd taken your time."

When she remained silent, he realized that she had fallen fast asleep. Kissing her cheek, he rolled them to their sides, pulled the comforter around them and held her close. He wasn't sure how he was going to explain why he hadn't been entirely honest with her about owning the ranch or the fact that neither of them would ever have to work another day in their lives if they didn't want to.

But it was past time he told her everything about himself and the reasons he'd felt compelled to keep the information from her. He hoped she'd understand his past experience with his gold-digging stepmother and the years she'd held his family's ranch hostage in her attempt to get the most money she could out of it. He also hoped Karly would be able to do the same when he told her about that buckle bunny, the one claiming he had made her pregnant in an effort to extort money from him, and how it had left him deeply suspicious of women's motives, as well.

When she murmured his name and snuggled into his embrace, he kissed her forehead. He wasn't sure how she would react to his revelations. But tomorrow he was going to tell her everything, pray that she understood and ask her to stay with him for the rest of his life.

The morning after the barbecue at the Laughlins', Karly sat at the table in the mansion's library, staring at the screen on Blake's laptop. She was supposed to be finishing up a purchase order for novelty items from one of the import companies in Hong Kong. But she couldn't have cared less about cases of rubber ducks, plush finger puppets and inflatable plastic beach balls. Her mind was on what would happen at the end of the week when it was time for her to leave the Wolf Creek Ranch. Blake hadn't mentioned anything about wanting them to stay married and have her remain in Wyoming with him. And she hadn't told him that she would like to stay and be his wife.

Nibbling on her lower lip, she thought about her reasons for refusing to join him at the ranch after they left Las Vegas and how she felt about that now. After she and Blake parted eight months ago, she had returned to pack up her apartment and quit her job. And that had been when her doubts set in. She had worried that she might move to the ranch and discover that she couldn't stand the quiet remoteness or that she would miss having a productive career. She had been so afraid of being unhappy that she'd convinced herself not to even take the chance.

But now that she'd spent time on the ranch, she found that she loved the peace and quiet. And it came as no small surprise that she found feeding a couple of orphaned calves much more rewarding than keeping a warehouse stocked with rubber ducks and plastic beach balls.

She sighed. She'd watched her mother sink into a deep depression after they returned to New York from the Midwest, especially after Martina hadn't been able to resume her career in the fashion industry. Her mother's misery had left a lasting impression on Karly and one of her biggest fears had always been that she would turn out to be as dissatisfied and resentful as her mother.

But looking at things objectively, Karly could never remember a time when her mother had been truly happy—not before they'd moved to the Midwest or after. Martina Ewing had been dissatisfied before her husband moved them away from New York. She'd been unhappy living in a small town in Middle America and when she and Karly returned to New York, she hadn't been content there, either. It was a hard truth to face, but her mother had been one of those people who always searched for something to make her happy and when she couldn't find it, blamed someone else. She had never discovered that true happiness comes from within and that just being with the people she loved was a real blessing.

But this time with Blake had convinced Karly of that truth. No matter where they lived or whatever job she needed to work to help with their finances, she knew she would be truly fulfilled as long as they were together. And she finally felt ready to create a life of happiness with him. She hoped he was ready for that, too.

"You wouldn't happen to know where Blake is, would you?" a man's voice asked from just inside the door.

Unaware there was anyone else around, Karly jumped and placed her hand on her chest as if that would slow down her racing heart. "Oh, dear heavens!"

"I'm sorry," the man said, stepping forward with his hands outstretched in front of him as if to stop her from panicking. "I didn't mean to frighten you." He looked contrite as he hooked his thumb over his shoulder toward the hall. "I would have asked Silas, but he's taking his afternoon nap and it's easier to wake the dead than to try to rouse him once he's asleep."

"Silas does seem to be able to sleep through anything." She'd noticed that fact while working to set up her workspace in the library a couple of days ago. Feeling calmer, Karly smiled. "Blake is out in the arena working with a new stallion."

The man nodded. "Thanks." He turned to leave, then turned back. "By the way, I'm Sean Hartwell, Blake's brother."

Once he'd introduced himself, she could immediately see the resemblance between the two men. About the same height, Sean had the same dark brown hair and brown eyes as Blake.

"I'm Karly Ewing," she said, not sure if Blake had mentioned he had a wife.

"Are you his new secretary or assistant?" Sean asked.

She wondered why Blake would need an assistant. It suddenly dawned on her that Sean must have meant to ask if she was the ranch owner's new secretary.

Smiling, she shook her head. "No, I'm staying with Blake for a few days over at the foreman's cottage."

Sean surprised her when he frowned. "Why are the two of you staying over there? He hasn't lived there since he built this place and moved in almost two years ago."

Karly stared at Sean for several long moments as reality began to sink in. "I-I'm not sure," she said slowly. "I suppose you'll have to ask him."

"You can count on it," he said, nodding.

"Do you and Blake own the ranch together?" she asked, feeling as if she had a knot the size of her fist in her stomach.

"No. My ranch is about forty-five minutes away on the other side of the ridge," he said, apparently unaware of his brother's ruse. He pointed toward the laptop on the library table. "I'll let you get back to whatever it is you're doing. It was nice to meet you, Karly. I hope you enjoy the rest of your visit to the Wolf Creek."

"It was nice to meet you, too, Sean," she murmured when he turned toward the door.

As she watched him leave, her chest tightened and it was extremely difficult to draw air into her lungs. Why would Blake lie to her? Why hadn't he told her he owned the Wolf Creek Ranch when they were in Las Vegas?

Of course they hadn't talked about much of anything personal. But that didn't explain why he had failed to tell her when she arrived to have him sign the new set of divorce papers.

A cold wave of sadness suddenly swept over her. He hadn't asked her to sign a prenuptial agreement. When she told him it would be best for them to end their marriage, Blake had obviously been afraid she would try to get part of his ranch.

She looked around the library and it became crystal clear that Blake had to be extremely wealthy. Log homes were some of the most expensive types of houses to build and one the size of this mansion would cost several millions of dollars just for the construction. The custom-built furnishings for a place this size would cost at least that much more. Then there was the pool area, with its waterfalls and tropical oasis hot tub. No telling how much that cost. Factor in a huge indoor arena and heated stable, the house and barns down the road and thousands of acres of land…

"Oh, my God," she said, sinking back down onto the chair at the table. "He thought I would try to take…" She covered her mouth with her hand to hold back a sob. His assets and hanging on to them was obviously more important to him than telling her the truth. He hadn't even given her the opportunity to assure him she had no interest in taking anything away from him.

Yes, she'd broken her promise to him when she'd asked for a divorce, but never once had she deliberately lied to him.

Standing up, she hurried into the foyer, threw open the massive front door, ran out to the ranch truck Blake had been using and got into the driver's seat. He made a habit of leaving the keys in the ignition whenever they were on ranch land and she was thankful he did.

When she started the truck and drove down the lane to the road, she didn't look back in the rearview mirror. Blake had made it crystal clear there was nothing back there for her.

She'd made her own mistakes by giving into her fears and not telling him the real reason behind her asking for a divorce. But what he'd done had been far worse. He had deliberately misled her and had no intention of asking her to stay with him to see if they could work things out. He'd probably been relieved when she called to tell him she wouldn't be moving to Wyoming with him. That would certainly explain why he hadn't been more insistent that she give their marriage a chance.

Tears streamed down her cheeks as she drove the short distance to the foreman's cottage, she went inside to retrieve the things she'd brought with her from Seattle and loaded the rental car. It was just as well that she'd found out about his ruse. Even if he had finally come clean about what he'd been trying so hard to hide, she didn't think she would ever be able to trust him.

Sobbing, she drove down the mountain road toward Eagle Fork. She hadn't been after his ranch, his money or anything material. Whether Blake was as rich as sin or as poor as a pauper, all she'd ever wanted, all she'd ever cared about, was having him love her.

"Hey there, bro," Blake said, riding the stallion over to where Sean stood just inside the arena doors. "You missed a great party last night over at the Rusty Spur."

His brother nodded. "I was on my way back from a situation up in Sheridan."

"Anything you can talk about?" Blake asked.

"Some guy is robbing banks all over the state and I was asked to review the details of his latest robbery," Sean answered.

"If he's been at this a while, I'm surprised they haven't called you in before now," Blake commented.

"This was the first time somebody got killed," Sean answered.

When his brother fell silent, Blake knew that was all Sean would say on the matter. Blake wasn't surprised that Sean didn't go into more detail about the case. He never talked about the work he did for the FBI and Blake never pressed for more than his brother was willing to tell.

"So what are you up to this afternoon?" Blake asked, dismounting the horse.

"I came by to see if you want to go fishing with me tomorrow." His brother shrugged. "But after I met your houseguest, I decided you probably wouldn't be interested."

"You met Karly?" Blake asked, hoping the subject of who owned the ranch hadn't been a topic of conversation.

"Yeah, she seems real nice," Sean commented. "But why are you two staying over at the homestead?"

"It's...complicated." A knot began to form in his gut as he realized Karly must have mentioned where they were staying. He asked, "Did you mention that I own the ranch?"

Sean stared at him for what seemed like forever before he finally nodded. "She asked and I wasn't going to lie to her." When Blake cut loose with a string of cusswords that had his brother raising his eyebrows, Sean asked, "Care to explain what brought on that little display of profanity?"

"Have one of the men take care of Blaze," Blake said, handing Sean the stallion's reins.

"What's going on?" Sean demanded when Blake took off across the yard toward the house.

"I'll tell you later," he called over his shoulder. "I have to go talk to my wife."

Blake knew he would face an interrogation from Sean later on but he'd worry about that when the time came. Right now, he needed to talk to Karly and explain why he hadn't told her everything months ago.

Running across the patio, Blake started calling her name as soon as he entered the house. When his calls went unanswered an icy dread began to settle in the pit of his stomach.

His heart stalled when he went into the foyer and found the front door ajar. Looking out, he really couldn't say he was surprised to see the ranch truck gone and along with it, his wife.

By the time he went back inside to get the keys for one of the vehicles in the garage, his brother met him in the kitchen. "What the hell's going on?" Sean demanded.

"I don't have time to get into it," Blake said, heading over to the key rack. "I have to get over to the foreman's cottage to stop Karly."

"My truck's out front," Sean said, starting for the door. "Come on, I'll drive you over there. And on the way you can explain when you got a wife and why she didn't have a clue that you own this spread."

As they drove away, Blake explained about their marriage in Vegas, Karly showing up with the new set of divorce papers and his reasoning behind not telling her up front that he was more than a ranch foreman and part-time rodeo rider. "I had planned on telling her when she moved here, right after Vegas. Then there seemed to be no real reason to share the truth, when we were headed for divorce. After the past few days... I had planned to tell her everything this evening after supper and ask her to stay with me."

His brother nodded. "Sorry I spoiled your reveal."

Blake shook his head. "Not your fault. I knew I was running out of time." He groaned as Sean parked beside the ranch truck. The little red sports car was gone. "She's headed back to Washington." He paused as he tried to think. "I'm just not sure if she's headed for Seattle or Lincoln County."

"What's in Lincoln County?" Sean asked.

"The divorce court," Blake answered, explaining the reason Karly intended to file there instead of in Seattle.

"Let me make a couple of phone calls," Sean said, reaching for his cell phone.

Blake knew if there was any chance of finding Karly, Sean had the connections to do it. But finding her was only half the battle. Getting her to listen to him was an entirely different matter.

While his brother tried to track down where Karly was headed, Blake went into the foreman's cottage to see if Karly had taken her luggage. He wasn't surprised to see that she'd taken the things she'd brought with her, but left the clothing, hat and boots he'd bought for her on their shopping trip to the Blue Sage Western Emporium.

Blake walked back downstairs and met Sean on the back porch. "She just called Cheyenne and made reservations for a flight to Denver. From there she's headed to Seattle."

Blake took a deep breath. He'd caught a break. "What time does her flight leave Denver?"

"Not until around six this evening," Sean

said, grinning. "She's going to miss the earlier afternoon flight by about an hour."

Blake checked his watch. "Can you get me down there to catch that early flight?"

His brother snorted. "If I can't, I'll turn in my license to fly helicopters." Sean had earned his pilot's license during his stint in the marines and because of his work with the FBI, regularly flew himself into Denver to catch flights to wherever there was a situation in need of his expertise.

Without another word, they both headed for Sean's truck. As his brother drove toward his ranch on the other side of the western ridge surrounding the Wolf Creek Ranch, Blake called to reserve a seat on the earlier flight to Seattle.

He didn't have a clear-cut plan, but he wasn't overly concerned. He had several hours before Karly's flight arrived and by then, he had no doubt he'd have something in mind.

When Karly called eight months ago, he'd told himself he was doing the right thing when he let her go without putting up a fight. It was what she wanted and he'd reasoned that pushing her would have done nothing to change her mind. But he wasn't going to make that mistake again. This time he was going to pull out all the stops.

He had no idea how long it would take to convince her, but one thing was certain. Blake wasn't returning to the Wolf Creek Ranch without her.

Nine

As Karly walked through the terminal toward the baggage claim area, she watched people as they met up with their loved ones and friends. It seemed that everyone else had someone there waiting to greet them. As usual, she had no one.

Tears threatened and she blinked several times to chase them away. It had never bothered her that she didn't have anyone to welcome her home after a trip. She had always collected her luggage, caught a cab and hadn't thought twice about being alone.

But that had changed with her trip to Wyoming. She'd never felt more alone in her entire life than she did at the moment.

Picking up her bag, she had to admit that wasn't quite true. The only other time she had felt such a keen sense of loneliness had been eight months ago when she'd returned from her vacation in Las Vegas and she was facing the night alone without Blake to hold her.

Her breath caught on a sob and she hurried out of the exit to the line of yellow cabs, waiting to take travelers to their destinations. While the driver stored her bag in the trunk, she settled into the backseat and prayed that the man wasn't overly chatty. She really didn't think she could talk to anyone without making a fool of herself. All she wanted to do was go home to her apartment away from the prying eyes of strangers and cry herself into oblivion. Thankfully it was dark enough that even if she did lose control, chances were the man wouldn't notice.

When they reached her apartment complex, she paid the cabdriver and pulled her travel bag along behind her as she slowly walked the short distance to her ground-floor apartment. But once she approached the door, she spotted a man sitting in the shadows on her porch step. Unsure whether to proceed and demand that he leave or turn around and run for help, she stopped dead in her tracks. That's when he looked up.

Her heart pounded and drawing a breath was all but impossible. "Blake?"

"This isn't safe," he said, shaking his head. "There should be lights along these sidewalks and dusk-to-dawn security lights on every building."

"I left the front-door light on," she said defensively. "It must have burned out."

"I don't like you living in a place where the security is this lax," he said, rising to his feet as he looked around.

"Oh, really?" She shook her head as she reached inside her handbag for her key. "How safe it is where I live isn't any of your concern anymore."

"Like hell!" When she pulled the key from her bag, he took it from her trembling fingers and unlocked and opened the door for her. "You're my wife. Your safety is of the utmost importance to me."

His attitude and his reference to her as his wife infuriated and broke her heart at the same time. How could he claim to want the best for her when he hadn't trusted her with the truth?

"Get real, Blake." She brushed past him to

enter her apartment and turn on one of the lamps at the end of the couch. "The most important things in your life are your precious ranch and your bank account. I doubt that I even make the top ten on your list of things you value."

"That's not true," he said, following her into her small living room. "You're more important to me than my next breath."

"Whatever," she said, dropping her purse on the coffee table. She turned to face him. "I don't know why you're here or what you think you're going to accomplish by following me to Seattle, but—"

"I came to talk to my wife," he said, closing the door behind him.

"I don't see that there's anything left to say." She shook her head. "You had ample opportunity to talk to me while I was at the Wolf Creek Ranch and you chose not to. And stop calling me your wife."

"I'm here now to set things straight," he said stubbornly crossing his arms. He stood like a stone statue and she realized he had every intention of making her listen to what he had to say. "And why shouldn't I call you my wife?" he asked. "We're still married."

She rubbed at the tension, causing her temples to pound unmercifully. "Please leave, Blake. I'm exhausted and you're not helping my developing headache."

He took a step toward her. "Sweetheart, I'm—"

"Don't call me that," she said, shaking her head as she backed away from him. "That's an endearment and one that you obviously don't mean and never have." She took a deep breath. "Now, will you please leave and go back to Wyoming, where you belong."

"I belong where you are." He walked over and sat down on the couch. "And I'm not leaving until we work this out."

Frustrated with his persistence to the point of tears she absolutely refused to let him see, she pulled her travel bag to the bedroom door. "I'm not going to argue with you any longer. I'm going to bed and I would prefer that you're gone when I get up in the morning. Please lock the door on your way out."

Without looking back, she walked into the bedroom, closed and locked the door, then leaned back against it. She couldn't imagine what Blake thought he could say to explain his actions or why he even cared to try. On the flight back to Seattle, she'd faced the brutal reality of the situation. No matter what he'd told her, Blake had never intended for their marriage to work. He'd never even told her what his life in Wyoming was really like! For that matter, she couldn't imagine why he'd married her to begin with. He'd probably been immensely relieved when she'd refused to join him on the ranch eight months ago.

It suddenly occurred to her that he might be here now to make sure she wasn't going to go after his money or try to take part of his ranch. The divorce wasn't final yet, after all.

"He doesn't need to worry," she murmured as she walked into the adjoining bathroom to brush her teeth. Even if he offered her a settlement, she would tell him what he could do with it. She had never wanted anything from him but his love, his respect and his honesty.

But even though he hadn't given her any of that, her heart had stalled and she'd barely resisted the urge to run into his arms when she first saw him sitting on her step. Nothing would have made her happier than to have him hold her close and tell her that it would all be all right and they could work things out.

As she looked in the mirror at the miserable woman staring back at her, Karly couldn't help but wonder if she'd lost her mind. How could Blake possibly look so darned good to her when he was the last person in the world she should want to see? Or trust?

Sitting at the small table in Karly's breakfast nook, Blake shifted in his chair in an effort to relieve the kinks in his back from sleeping on her couch. Sometime around midnight, he'd decided the damn thing should be certified as an instrument of torture. Not only had both of his feet gone to sleep from hanging over the end of it, but there was also a definite sag in the middle that had his back feeling like it had been broken in several places.

But as uncomfortable as it had been, there was no way he was going to leave this apartment until she heard what he had to say—even if he had to sleep on that damn couch all week. After he'd laid it all on the line, then if she still wanted to kick him to the curb, he'd somehow find the strength to bow out of the picture— even if it killed him—and let her go. The bottom line was and always had been that he loved her and wanted nothing but her happiness. He could only hope that happiness included him.

"I thought you'd be gone by now," she said when she walked into the tiny kitchen carrying a box of tissues. Her eyes were red and puffy and he knew she'd spent most of the night cry-

ing. Just knowing he was the cause of her dis-
tress nearly killed him.

But as he continued to look at her, his heart
stalled. With her long blond hair slightly mussed
from sleep and wearing a nightshirt that was at
least two sizes too large and about as shapeless
as a tow sack, he didn't think he'd ever seen her
look sexier.

He took a sip of his coffee and shook his
head as he tried to focus on what he needed
to say to get her to listen. "I'm not going anywhere until we talk."

"I have to go to work," she said, placing the
box on the table and walking over to pour herself a cup of the coffee he'd made earlier.

"I'll be here when you get home." He
shrugged. "Whether it's now or later, we are
going to discuss this, Karly."

She stared at him for several long seconds
before she closed her eyes as if trying to find
patience. When she opened them, the emotional pain he detected in the blue depths just
about tore him apart. The thought that he was
the cause of that sadness was more than he
could bear.

"Blake, I don't know what you could possibly say that's going to make a difference," she
said, sinking into the chair across the table

from him. "You obviously didn't want me to know that you own the Wolf Creek Ranch or that you're quite wealthy."

Guilt settled across his shoulders. "Karly, there were a couple of reasons I didn't tell you about my assets when we first met."

"I remember you telling me about the owner's stepmother being a gold digger and how hard it was to get the ranch back," she said, sounding defeated. "I just wasn't aware you were talking about yourself and the difficulties you had with her. But I had nothing to do with that."

"I know." He slowly set his coffee cup on the table. "Sean and I had hints of the way she was after Dad married her, but when he passed away she took the gloves off and made it clear she was going to do everything she could to cut us out and keep us from inheriting anything she thought she could turn into cash."

"It's unfortunate that she turned out to be so ruthless and I can understand you becoming suspicious of other women's motives." Karly shook her head. "But I didn't know anything about you having money and you had no right to blame me for crimes I didn't commit. And for that matter, never would commit."

"I know, sweetheart, and I can't tell you how sorry I am for that."

He stared down at his loosely clasped hands resting on the table a moment before he took a deep breath and met her accusing gaze head-on. She needed to know all of the reasons behind his caution, even if those reasons were something he was less than proud of.

"I also had my own run-in with a woman several years back who tried to extort money from me," he said, cursing himself for being such a fool.

"Once again, I had nothing to do with that," she reminded him. He hadn't expected her to make his confession easy on him and he deserved nothing less than her condemnation.

"I realize that, but I owe you an explanation and an apology." He took a deep breath. "About six years ago, I was at a rodeo in San Antonio and won the bull-riding event. Instead of celebrating with a can of beer and a good night's sleep like I should have, I went out on the town."

"You got drunk," she said, cutting right to the heart of the matter.

Blake nodded. "Yeah. And I should have stopped with that and gone back to the hotel."

"But you didn't," she mused.

"No. I went back to a cheap motel close to

the bar." He hesitated. "I was with one of the buckle bunnies."

"What are those?" Karly asked, taking a sip from her coffee cup. Her doubtful expression hadn't changed, but she was at least showing an interest in his explanation.

"Rodeo groupies," he answered, wishing he'd never heard of them, either. "Some of them are harmless, but others want to sleep with rough stock riders who win."

"Why?" she asked, frowning.

"For the bragging rights," he said, disgusted with himself for falling into that trap. "It's like a feather in their cap to say they've slept with this or that rider." He shook his head at his foolishness. "Anyway, I spent the night with one of them and a month later she showed up claiming I had made her pregnant."

Karly's eyes widened. "You have a child?"

"Good God, no," he said hurriedly. "It turned out that she wasn't pregnant at all. She had asked around and found out that I had money and was in line to inherit at least part of the Wolf Creek Ranch. She decided I was an easy mark for a big payoff."

"She thought you would pay her to end the pregnancy?" Karly asked, looking affronted.

He nodded. "Just about the time I offered to

raise the baby on my own, I learned she wasn't pregnant and never had been."

Karly looked thoughtful for a moment as if she was processing what he had told her. "I suppose something like that would leave you with an overabundance of caution."

"It had been my experience not to let people know that I was more than just another dust-covered cowboy trying to make a living off riding bulls and herding cattle," he said, nodding. "Then I met you and before I found a way to tell you about myself, we got married and started making plans for you to move to the ranch."

"Why didn't you tell me then?" she asked, her tone accusing. "Was it because you failed to get me to sign a prenuptial agreement before the wedding ceremony?"

"Not at all." He had to make her understand. "I had plans to tell you when you joined me at the ranch. I thought it would be a nice surprise learning that we'd never have to worry about finances the way other couples do when they first start out. You'd have the option of continuing with your career, work part-time or quit and be a full-time ranch wife. Whatever you wanted to do."

"Only I called and told you that if we stayed

married, you'd have to move to Seattle," she said slowly.

"Yeah." He stared down at his empty cup. When he looked up, he added, "But I wasn't the only one with a secret, was I?"

"What do you mean?" she asked, frowning. "I've always been honest with you."

"Sweetheart, from what you've told me about your parents and their divorce, I think that carried a lot of weight in your decision not to come to Wyoming eight months ago." He reached across the table to cover her delicate hand with his. "The only thing I don't know is how it influenced you and why."

She had opened up about her parents during their conversation in the hot tub and he was positive their divorce had somehow played into her choices about them. But he needed to know how their problems had become her problems. How were they holding her back?

When Karly remained silent, he got up to round the table. He picked her up and sat down with her on his lap. "I know I screwed up by not telling you everything about myself and the reasons I felt I had to be cautious. But you've left out some important information about yourself, too. What we've got is good and worth fighting for, Karly. Talk to me. Tell me what held you back and why you were so frightened—why you're still frightened."

"You won't understand," she said quietly. She shook her head. "I'm not even sure it makes sense."

"Why don't you tell me and maybe we can make sense of it together?" he suggested, loving that she was in his arms again and wasn't pushing away from him.

She remained silent for a minute before she finally spoke. "From the moment we moved to the Midwest my mother hated it and before it was over with, she despised my father as well." She turned her head to give him a pointed look. "After she and I moved back to New York she blamed him for everything that went wrong in her life—the loss of her career, her unhappiness. Sometimes I even think she didn't like me because I was part of him."

When she fell silent, Blake kissed her cheek and hugged her close. "I'm sure she loved you, sweetheart."

She shrugged one slender shoulder. "Whether she did or not, I was afraid that if I discovered I didn't like living outside of a city the same thing would happen to us." Tears filled her blue eyes when she looked at him. "I care too much for you to let that happen, Blake. You deserved better than to be resented and blamed for something you had no control over."

Giving her a kiss that left them both breathless, he raised his head to smile at her. "I love you, too, sweetheart. I always have and I always will."

That was all it took for the floodgates to open and when she lay her head on his shoulder, Blake held her while her tears ran their course. He hated seeing a woman cry, but Karly's tears were especially gut-wrenching. She was crying for the child who had doubted her mother's love, as well as what her parents' mistakes had almost cost the two of them.

When she raised her head he handed her a tissue from the box on the table. "Feel better now?" he asked, smiling at the only woman he had ever loved.

Her cheeks turned a rosy pink. "I'm sorry. I hate being so emotional."

"You don't have to apologize to me, Karly," he said, kissing her forehead. "It's my job to be here for you during the bad times, as well as the good."

"I love you so much, Blake," she said, throwing her arms around his neck.

"And I love you, Karly," he said, hugging her tightly against him.

They sat that way for some time, content just to be in each other's arms.

"So where are we going to live?" he finally asked.

She sat back to give him a strange look. "I… assume we'll live in Wyoming at your ranch."

"Only if that's where you want to live," he assured her. "As long as I have you, I'll live anywhere and make a trip back to the ranch periodically."

"Blake, I was wrong," she said, placing her soft palms on his cheeks to gaze into his eyes. "I love your ranch."

"Our ranch," he amended. "It's yours now, as much as it is mine."

She shook her head. "All I want is you."

"Do you really want to argue about this now?" he asked, laughing.

Smiling, she shook her head. "I want to live with you on the Wolf Creek Ranch. That's where I want to ride Suede and help you feed bucket babies and raise our own babies." Her smile faded. "I know we haven't talked about it, but you do want a family, don't you?"

"There are a lot of things we haven't talked about," he said, nodding. "But now that you're coming home with me, we have plenty of time to share our hopes and dreams." When she continued to look at him, he grinned. "Yes, Karly. I want a family and I'll be more than happy to give you all the babies you want."

"I love you so much," she said, snuggling against him. "I can't wait to go back home."

His chest tightened with emotion at her reference to the ranch as home. "There's something else I intended to do for you after we got married in Vegas."

"What's that?" she asked, kissing his neck.

Her lips sent a flash fire blazing through his veins and he had to take a deep breath in order to answer her. "The ceremony we had in Vegas wasn't very fancy and I want to see that you have the wedding of your dreams."

"Oh, Blake, I would love that," she said, tears filling her eyes once again. "But we'll have to wait until spring."

He frowned. "Why would we have to do that?"

"I'd really like to renew our vows out on the patio by the waterfall," she said, looking hopeful. "I think it would be beautiful if we could have a sunset wedding."

"We can make that happen," he said, nodding. "It's warm enough right now. How about this coming weekend?"

"We don't have time to arrange everything," she said, looking doubtful.

"Sweetheart, you'd be surprised how quickly things can be arranged when you have the money to do it," he said, laughing.

"How about the following weekend?" she asked. "I really need time to think about what I want."

"That sounds good to me," he said, standing up with her in his arms.

"Where are we going?" she asked as he carried her across the living room.

"I'm going to take my wife into her bedroom and make love to her," he said, kissing her soundly. "Then while you go to work, I'm going to try to get some sleep. Do you know how uncomfortable that damned couch is?"

Her laughter was one of the sweetest sounds he'd ever heard. "After we make love, I'm going to call and tell my boss that I won't be coming back. Then I'm going to stay in bed and take a nap because I didn't get much sleep last night, either."

As he placed her on the bed and stretched out beside her, Blake kissed her soft, perfect lips. "Are you sure you want to quit your job, Karly? I don't want you doing anything you might regret."

"I'm positive." She reached for the snaps on his chambray shirt. "Now, will my husband please make love to me?"

They could plan their wedding and discuss her decision to quit her job later. Right now, he had his beautiful wife asking him to make love to her and she wasn't going to have to ask him twice.

"I love you, Karly Ewing Hartwell. You own me, heart and soul."

"And I love you, Blake. More than you'll ever know."

Epilogue

Two weeks later, as Karly stood in front of the mirror in the bedroom she'd used at the foreman's cottage, she waited for Tori Laughlin to work the tiny buttons through the decorative loops at the back of her long, white satin and lace strapless wedding gown. "Is Eli here with the carriage?" she asked.

"He just arrived," Tori answered, finishing with the buttons on Karly's dress. She walked over and picked up the veil they'd laid out on the bed earlier. "Thank heavens Blake got the road asphalted these past two weeks. I'd hate to see your beautiful dress covered in Wyoming dust."

Karly nodded. "I couldn't believe how quickly the crew from the construction company finished surfacing the road from here to the main house."

"It doesn't take long," Tori said as she pinned the tulle and lace to the back of Karly's loosely upswept hair. When Karly's new best friend stepped back, she smiled. "You're going to knock the socks off Blake when he sees you in this."

"That's the plan," Karly said, smiling as she looked at herself in the full length mirror.

After she and Blake returned to the ranch from Seattle, Karly had gone into full wedding mode and, with Tori's recommendation, hired a wedding planner from Cheyenne. The woman had been nothing short of a miracle worker and once Karly had told her what she wanted and the date, all that had been left for Karly to do was decide on the perfect dress. Fortunately, she found what she wanted at the first bridal shop she and Tori visited and once the alterations were completed there really hadn't been all that much for her to do.

A knock on the door signaled that it was time for Eli to drive them over to the main house for the ceremony that would renew Karly and Blake's wedding vows. When Tori opened

the door he grinned. "You ladies look beautiful." Eli kissed his wife. "Blake and I are the
two luckiest guys this side of the Great Di-
vide."

"And don't you forget it," Tori said, kissing her husband's cheek. Turning to Karly, she
asked, "Are you ready?"

"I'm more than ready," Karly said, picking
up the bouquet the wedding planner had de-
livered earlier.

As they made their way downstairs and out
to the white horse-drawn carriage that would
take them over to the main house for the ceremony, Karly couldn't stop smiling. She felt
a little like Cinderella and knowing that her
very own Prince Charming would be waiting
to help her down from the carriage once they
arrived at the ranch house made her impatient
to get there. She hadn't seen Blake since earlier in the day when Tori arrived to take them
to get their hair and nails done down in Eagle
Fork and she'd missed him terribly.

When Eli drove the carriage up the drive to
the log mansion, Karly's breath caught at the
sight of Blake waiting for them at the end of
the sidewalk leading to the patio. Dressed in
a Western cut tuxedo, black snake-skin boots

and a wide brimmed black hat, he truly was the man of her dreams.

"You're gorgeous," he whispered close to her ear as he lifted her down from the carriage.

"You clean up real nice yourself, cowboy," Karly said, rising on tiptoes to kiss his lean cheek.

"Are you ready to become Mrs. Hartwell?" he asked as he tucked her hand in the crook of his arm and started walking toward the waterfall where the minister and his brother Sean were waiting on them.

"I'm already Mrs. Hartwell," she said, loving her new last name.

He nodded. "But this time it's permanent, sweetheart."

As she glanced toward the Western sky, the sun was just beginning to sink behind the mountain peaks and it was time for her sunset wedding to begin. "I've never been more ready for anything in my entire life," she said as they walked past over a hundred guests assembled on the patio.

As the last of their wedding guests drove away from the ranch house, Blake took Karly in his arms and kissed her until she sagged against him. "I've got a surprise for you," he said, taking her by the hand to lead her around to the other side of the pool.

When he stopped by the fire pit where he'd lain a small amount of kindling, the woman he loved more than life itself looked up at him like he'd lost every ounce of sense he possessed. "Seriously? Do you really want to build a fire now?"

Happier than he'd ever been, he grinned. "Trust me. I think you'll like this."

"I was looking forward to going upstairs to give you a wedding surprise of my own," she said as she continued to stare at him.

"I promise this won't take long," he said, lighting the dry wood. When the fire began to crackle, Blake reached into the inside pocket of his tuxedo and pulled out an envelope. "I thought we could get rid of these together."

A look of understanding sparkled in her pretty blue eyes and a smile curved her lips. "The divorce papers. I had forgotten all about them."

"I hadn't," he said, removing the documents from the envelope. He gave them to her, then just as they'd done when they cut their wedding cake, he covered her hand with his and they tossed them onto the fire together.

As they watched the papers curl and turn

black as they burned, Blake held Karly close. "Now that we have that taken care of, what's this about you having a gift for me?"

Her lovely smile sent his blood pressure sky-high. "You'll have to wait until early summer for the actual gift. But I can tell you about it."

He leaned forward to press his lips to hers. "I'm listening."

"It's going to be small and loud at times," she said, grinning. "And you're probably going to lose a lot of sleep because of it."

Blake had no idea where she was going with this, but she definitely had his full attention. "Okay," he said cautiously. "Would you like to tell me what *it* is?"

"I don't know yet." Something about the look in her eyes caused the air to lodge in his lungs a moment before she grinned. "But as soon as we find out, we'll be redecorating the room across the hall from the master suite in either pink or blue."

"You're pregnant."

"No, we're pregnant," she said, laughing. "*We* got me into this together and *we're* going to get me out of it. Together."

He suddenly couldn't stop grinning and he was pretty sure he looked like a damned fool.

He couldn't have cared less. They were going to have a baby.

Pulling her in his arms, he kissed her until they both gasped for breath. "It happened the morning we worked things out."

She nodded. "We were so caught up in the moment, that's the only time we forgot about protection."

"I love you, Karly Hartwell," he said around the lump clogging his throat.

When he swung her up into his arms and started toward the house, she cupped his face with her soft palm. "And I love you, Blake. Now, please take me upstairs so I can show you just how much."

* * * * *

If you liked this tale of strong, sexy cowboys, pick up THE GOOD, THE BAD AND THE TEXAN *series from* USA TODAY *bestselling author Kathie DeNosky:*

HIS MARRIAGE TO REMEMBER
A BABY BETWEEN FRIENDS
YOUR RANCH...OR MINE?
THE COWBOY'S WAY
PREGNANT WITH THE RANCHER'S BABY
TEMPTED BY THE TEXAN

Available now from Harlequin Desire!

* * *

If you're on Twitter, tell us what you think of Harlequin Desire! #harlequindesire

#2473 THE RANCHER RETURNS
The Westmoreland Legacy • by Brenda Jackson
When a Navy SEAL returns home, he finds a sexy professor digging up his ranch in search of treasure! He wants her off his land...and in his arms! But his family's secrets may stand in the way of seduction...

#2474 THE BLACK SHEEP'S SECRET CHILD
Billionaires and Babies • by Cat Schield
When his brother's widow comes to Trent Caldwell asking him to save the family company, he knows exactly what he wants in return. First, complete control of the business. Then the secretive single mother back in his bed...

#2475 THE PREGNANCY PROPOSITION
Hawaiian Nights • by Andrea Laurence
When plain Paige flies to a Hawaiian resort to fulfill her grandfather's dying wish, she's tempted by the hotel's handsome owner. Will her unplanned pregnancy ruin their chance at giving in to more than desire?

#2476 HIS SECRET BABY BOMBSHELL
Dynasties: The Newports • by Jules Bennett
After their secret affair, Graham Newport discovers Eva Winchester is pregnant! Her father is Graham's most hated business rival, but he's ready to fight for Eve and their baby...as long as he can keep his heart out of the negotiations!

#2477 CONVENIENT COWGIRL BRIDE
Red Dirt Royalty • by Silver James
Chase Barron needs a wife without pesky emotional expectations. Down-on-her-luck cowgirl Savannah Wolfe needs help getting back on the rodeo circuit. A marriage of convenience may solve both their problems—unless they fall in love...

#2478 HIS ILLEGITIMATE HEIR
The Beaumont Heirs • by Sarah M. Anderson
Zeb Richards has never wanted anything more than he wants the Beaumont's prized company. Until he meets top employee Casey Johnson. Now this boss is breaking all the rules for just one night—a night with consequences...

REQUEST YOUR FREE BOOKS!
2 FREE NOVELS PLUS 2 FREE GIFTS!

⊕HARLEQUIN®

Desire

ALWAYS POWERFUL, PASSIONATE AND PROVOCATIVE

YES! Please send me 2 FREE Harlequin® Desire novels and my 2 FREE gifts (gifts are worth about $10). After receiving them, if I don't wish to receive any more books, I can return the shipping statement marked "cancel." If I don't cancel, I will receive 6 brand-new novels every month and be billed just $4.55 per book in the U.S. or $5.24 per book in Canada. That's a savings of at least 13% off the cover price! It's quite a bargain! Shipping and handling is just 50¢ per book in the U.S. and 75¢ per book in Canada.* I understand that accepting the 2 free books and gifts places me under no obligation to buy anything. I can always return a shipment and cancel at any time. Even if I never buy another book, the two free books and gifts are mine to keep forever.

225/326 HDN GH2P

Name	(PLEASE PRINT)
Address	Apt. #
City	State/Prov.	Zip/Postal Code

Signature (if under 18, a parent or guardian must sign)

Mail to the **Reader Service:**
IN U.S.A.: P.O. Box 1867, Buffalo, NY 14240-1867
IN CANADA: P.O. Box 609, Fort Erie, Ontario L2A 5X3

Want to try two free books from another line?
Call 1-800-873-8635 or visit www.ReaderService.com.

* Terms and prices subject to change without notice. Prices do not include applicable taxes. Sales tax applicable in N.Y. Canadian residents will be charged applicable taxes. Offer not valid in Quebec. This offer is limited to one order per household. Not valid for current subscribers to Harlequin Desire books. All orders subject to credit approval. Credit or debit balances in a customer's account(s) may be offset by any other outstanding balance owed by or to the customer. Please allow 4 to 6 weeks for delivery. Offer available while quantities last.

Your Privacy—The Reader Service is committed to protecting your privacy. Our Privacy Policy is available online at www.ReaderService.com or upon request from the Reader Service.

We make a portion of our mailing list available to reputable third parties that offer products we believe may interest you. If you prefer that we not exchange your name with third parties, or if you wish to clarify or modify your communication preferences, please visit us at www.ReaderService.com/consumerschoice or write to us at Reader Service Preference Service, P.O. Box 9062, Buffalo, NY 14240-9062. Include your complete name and address.

Navy SEAL Gavin Blake has returned home to the ranch he loves to make sure beautiful Layla Harris leaves his family's spread...

Read on for a sneak peek at
THE RANCHER RETURNS,
by New York Times *bestselling author*
Brenda Jackson,
the first in **THE WESTMORELAND LEGACY** *series!*

Gavin grabbed his duffel from the truck. He tilted his Stetson back on his head and looked at the car parked in front of his grandmother's guest cottage. Gavin hoped his grandmother hadn't extended an invitation for that professor to stay on their property as well as dig on their land. He didn't want anyone taking advantage of his family.

He'd taken one step onto the porch when the front door swung open and his grandmother walked out. She was smiling, and when she opened her arms, he dropped his duffel bag and walked straight into the hug awaiting him.

"Welcome home, Gavin," she said. "I didn't expect you for a few months yet. Did everything go okay?"

He smiled. She always asked him the same thing, knowing full well that because of the classified nature of his job as a SEAL, he couldn't tell her anything. "Yes, Gramma Mel, everything went okay. I'm back because—"

He blinked, not sure he was seeing straight. A woman stood in the doorway, but she wasn't just *some* woman. She had to be the most gorgeous woman he'd ever seen. Hell, she looked like everything he'd ever fantasized a woman to be, even while fully clothed in jeans and a pullover sweater.

Gavin studied her features, trying to figure out what had him spellbound. Was it the caramel-colored skin, dark chocolate eyes, dimpled cheeks, button nose or well-defined, kissable lips? Maybe every single thing.

Not waiting for his grandmother to make introductions, his mouth eased into a smile. He reached out his hand and said, "Hello, I'm Gavin."

The moment their hands touched, a jolt of desire shot through his body. Nothing like this had ever happened to him before. From the expression that flashed in her eyes, he knew she felt it, as well.

"It's nice meeting you, Gavin," she said softly. "Layla Harris."

Harris? His aroused senses suddenly screeched to a stop. Did she say *Harris*? Was Layla related to this Professor Harris? Was she part of the excavation team?

Now he had even more questions, and he was determined to get some answers.

Don't miss
THE RANCHER RETURNS
by New York Times *bestselling author Brenda Jackson*
available October 2016 wherever
Harlequin® Desire books and ebooks are sold.

www.Harlequin.com

Whatever You're Into... Passionate Reads

Looking for more passionate reads from Harlequin®?
Fear not! Harlequin® Presents, Harlequin® Desire and
Harlequin® Blaze offer you irresistible romance stories
featuring powerful heroes.

⬡HARLEQUIN® *Presents*®

Do you want alpha males, decadent glamour and jet-set
lifestyles? Step into the sensational, sophisticated world of
Harlequin® Presents, where sinfully tempting heroes ignite a
fierce and wickedly irresistible passion!

⬡HARLEQUIN® *Desire*

Harlequin® Desire novels are powerful, passionate and
provocative contemporary romances set against a backdrop of
wealth, privilege and sweeping family saga. Alpha heroes with
a soft side meet strong-willed but vulnerable heroines amid a
dramatic world of divided loyalties, high-stakes conflict and
intense emotion.

⬡HARLEQUIN® *Blaze*®

Harlequin® Blaze stories sizzle with strong heroines and
irresistible heroes playing the game of modern love and lust.
They're fun, sexy and always steamy.

Be sure to check out our full selection of books
within each series every month!

www.Harlequin.com

READERSERVICE.COM

Manage your account online!

- Review your order history
- Manage your payments
- Update your address

> *We've designed the*
> *Reader Service website*
> *just for you.*

Enjoy all the features!

- Discover new series available to you, and read excerpts from any series.
- Respond to mailings and special monthly offers.
- Connect with favorite authors at the blog.
- Browse the Bonus Bucks catalog and online-only exculsives.
- Share your feedback.

Visit us at:
ReaderService.com